Tursulowe Press, Philadelphia, PA
www.tursulowepress.com

ISBN 978-1-95-705719-4

Printed in the U.S.A.

beth kephart

TOMORROW WILL BRING SUNDAY'S NEWS

a philadelphia story

In loving memory of Margaret Finley D'Imperio

A novel is a mirror walking down the road.

— Michael Ondaatje, *The English Patient*
(or Stendhal by way of César Vichard de Saint-Réal)

She lies in her bed, in her room, listening:

the glug in the gutter. The calico across the narrow of the street, new to its own mew. October 21, 1969. Yesterday sound was the yellow fur of the sun behind the room where she lies. It was the sound of the basketball in the park past the alley, slapped against the ground so many times by an invisible hand that she would have done anything to crush it into silence, but what could she do? Who would carry her the distance, lift her head, find her words, and besides, it is raining now. The pleasing pattering of liquid weather.

Her mattress has been rutted by the long lengths of her illness. She feels, beneath her, the places her bones and flesh have been, the four depressions of the breakfast tray that her husband brought during the many months when she could still eat, or really just sip, a little. Beef broth. Orange-flavored Jell-O. Chocolate milk. Applesauce that her daughter made with the ripe McIntoshes and the hard sticks of cinnamon. *Here we are,* her husband would say, settling the pretty painted tray down among the white sheets, applying just enough pressure that the round feet of the wooden legs would become indelible in the deflated mattress.

Had he sat with her on the edge of the bed, the pretty painted would have gone sideways—lost its footing, tipped, released the bowl, the glass, the dish, the slosh onto the sheets he'd stopped washing, for she no longer had the strength to help him strip them from beneath her. To move to this side. To move to that side. To not get lost inside the puzzle of staying put but moving.

True, he might have brought the cushioned rocking chair with the string doily from the other room and sat right there, the two of them, together. He might have talked or hummed or listened, like she listened, to the weather. But that would have surprised them both, and they were long past surprises—the news of her illness being tired and ancient, his desire to keep living not—what is the word?—poignant? His desire to keep living was—here is the word—paramount.

A terrific paramounting wish. She makes new words now. Sluices others.

Besides: Whatever it was he'd cooked up for himself—pineapple ham, rosemary chicken, his famous meatballs and spaghetti—awaited (he was hungry) down the hallway, past the paintings, down the stairwell, in the dining room, the one room with the tall, wide window that looked out upon the alley, past the alley into the park. She's stopped picturing him alone at the big old table that never fit in that room to begin with. She's stopped thinking of the furniture that once held in a tight squeeze all the world that was theirs—their children, their grandchildren, their Thanksgiving, and their Easter. She'd been a woman who had laughed behind her hand. He'd been a man who'd saved enough, and proudly, for the pure gold tooth that replaced the broken molar. He'd smiled so that everyone could see it.

A cloth napkin tucked in at his pressed collar. His sleeves pulled up by the wide rubber bands at his elbows. An immaculate man. From the beginning of them. How little she ever learned about who he was before her.

She, too, had kept her secrets.

Not this thought. Not now. There is no time for wishing. There hardly ever was. She'd lived the alternate story, and this is the end of it.

The rain falls. It is her sound.

Her sigh barely lifts the bones of her chest.

Two days ago, the girl came to see her.

"Grandmom," she'd called, all the way up the steps, past the paintings, at the door.

Grandmom?

Her name like a question. The girl's love more promiscuous than her fear, though the fear will in time carry its own magnitudes, will fold and bend and corrugate the girl as she grows (one cheek more hollow than the other, sag in her flesh) into the one who will someday trust this story.

The girl knocking. The girl knocking at her bedroom door, which her husband had closed as if she were no longer fit for company, and she was not. Her legs were naked and white in the white of the sheets, and she could not lift herself to cover herself. The girl was only nine, and this would be the last time on this earth they would be seeing each other, and she did not wish to be seen like this—

but then—

The girl had bursted in—burst?—with her chopped bangs and her freckled face. The girl had seen her—naked as she was, uncovered.

Betty, she had tried to say.

Boop.

Her name for the girl who slammed the door shut and banged again from the other side, harder, frightened. *Grandmom.* She can't remember how the girl had gotten it done, but she did. The girl had walked back in to dignify her grandmother—covered her legs with the whites of the sheets, though turquoise would have been nice, or peach—peach sheets—for everything was fading, everything, in the end, is white.

Remembering the girl who had, just a few days ago, come. Remembering how the girl, more courageous now, had reached for her hand. The girl whose name is slipping—

Boop—

and then, in the very moment of the girl standing there, a blink of sun had clinked the silver handle of the brush that had been left on the dresser, her hair in its bristles. The sun had clinked, and the girl had turned to see, and she knew in that instant that the girl would always be like this, confusing her own senses, startled by them. She knew that she loved the girl even more for the verse she'd be, open and broken and wanting.

It tires her, remembering like this.

It tires, and appeases.

Now it is the sound of the song she hears, all of them singing her song. The Kit-Cat Band. Paul Whiteman. Louis Armstrong. Bing Crosby. Judy Garland. Frank Sinatra. Hoagy Carmichael. Joni James. Connie Francis. Everyone singing her song, the breath of it being hers, there on the Victrola, the song playing until the needle reached the dead wax on the run-out and time hitched and notched and someone stood and with elegant care returned the song to its start:

There's nothing left for me

Of days that used to be

Catalog number 358—the name and the sound and the shape of the song. Its place in history.

Just the rain keeping time in a world going white, going whiter, and now something altogether shifts, and time jumps its track, and it is years ago, when she herself is young, a girl and not a wife, a teen and not a sigher with a song.

A mind dying backwards.

Her sweater coat is emerald green

and worn all day, inside, outside. Peggy sits at the table in the kitchen at 1126 South Twenty-third Street, where the tea kettle steams and the cinnamon rises from the pie in the oven, because it is Tuesday, not Monday, and Tuesday, not Wednesday, meaning the city, in this hour, allows them heat and wheat.

She takes one hand out of its pocketed fist and churns the spare sprinkles of sugar in her cup with spoon, anticipating,

listening

past the window for the gull that blows in from the sea, pushed toward the city by the wind with one less feather in its wing. She is the tallest Finley, born 1902, waiting for news, which always arrives days late, passed house to house on South Twenty-third, the headlines landing with a whop on her three-stoned stoop and some of the words smudged off onto prior fingertips. She is careful not to stain the news, or lose it. In the wool well of her pocket the gull's feather sits, its vane neat, its rachis undiminished beside her second fist.

She'd found the feather yesterday. She'd snatched it for safekeeping.

The Germans, the French, the war. The shipbuilders at Hog Island. The women at Oxford Knitting Mill in Kensington knitting underwear for the combat men. Munitions at Baldwin. Words loose in their ink. Tomorrow Sunday's news will come.

The cinnamon steeps. The smell like a meal she would eat. The days falling crooked on the calendar of the week.

Through the cracks in time, she hears her name—Lani calling. Peggy laces up into her second-hand Hirsch-Ullman high-tops, polished just this morning with a buffing cloth, and cuts across the room, opens the door, and there Lani is, leaning out across a second-floor sill above the narrow of Twenty-third, her side.

"Been waiting on you," Lani says, impatient. Her head is pushed through the curtains so that her hair looks blue—smooth and blue with a fringe.

"Been busy," Peggy says, taking her seat on her three-step stoop, beside the broken grate. She is sixteen, a girl who has become the truest age, collecting feathers in the pockets of her sweater. She retrieves her latest Little Leather Library book, soft and green and sincerely leather, its binding delicate, its pages thin. "Ready?" she asks Lani, and Lani is, so Peggy begins. It's the Emerson. His essays.

"There is a time," Peggy reads, "in every man's education when he arrives at the conviction that envy is ignorance; that imitation is suicide; that he must take himself for better for worse as his portion; that though the wide universe is full of good, no kernel of nourishing corn can come to him but through his toil bestowed on that plot of ground which is given to him to till."

"*She*," Lani calls down from the sill across the narrow. "*Her.*"

"She," Peggy agrees. Also her. "Given to *her* to till."

"Go on," Lani says. Scratching the back of the cat. Lani, who doesn't know what's headed for her, who can't imagine what the men will do, how she almost will not make it home, how Peggy reading Emerson to her while she sits in a window with curtain fringe on her head will be the mark of her last youth.

In the actual world—the painful kingdom of time and place—dwell care and canker and fear.

The air is dark, and

the wind has gotten messed up with the rain. When it blows, what's left of her best song scatters, but not its ache. She wishes the girl would come back, but she's gone now, with her mother and her father and her brother and her sister, to the house on Maple Shade Lane, where the girl will live onward until she moves into a house Peggy will never see, marry a man she'll never meet, have a child she won't know, lose the pearl necklace that once was hers; it was her only legacy.

Boop, that's it. Betty Boop for Betsy for B—the real name that never fit; the girl had needed, from the start, a better name. *Boop*, she remembers saying, and the girl would come, skipping because she was a skipper, her short hair flopping *off* her forehead when she went up and flopping *onto* when she went down, wearing her Mary Janes, her thick cotton stockings bunched at her ankles like loose elephant skin.

The elephant at the zoo at 3400 West Girard, washing its back with a blow of dirt dust.

Remember?

She remembers.

She still has this—remembering.

"Sit with me," she would say, when the girl was so much younger, and the girl always did, the young heat of the girl crammed against the old heat of her cancer. Love wasn't hard, why was love always hard, love might have been just this: sitting the stoops with the girl she called Boop—Guyer Avenue, Burns Avenue, Wildwood Crest—and talking the small, humming—

Used to be—

There it is again. The rain claiming back the words of the song when the wind stops howling.

The grief—

Downstairs the man she married hoists his barrel belly from the front room to the middle room to the dining room with the wide window, then back to the dark middle room. When he chooses the chair where he'll sit he doesn't choose the chair where she'd once sat, listening to her song. She can hear him now, down below, practicing living without her, rushing the soles of his shoes *whish, whish* across the wood floor, then the muffle of the carpet, which she'd danced down to the bare threads when she wasn't sick like this. As sick. Then the wood floor again, its shine long gone. Then the threads.

Everything whitening except the parts that flare.

She had been, oh she had been, glamorous.

And the family?

What of them?

Where?

Working her mind into the facts of the past, past the painting of the girl with the two dark braids she had hung herself (a hammer in one hand, the nail between her teeth), through the distance to a day she can't remember in 1927, wearing a peach chiffon dress with a handkerchief skirt to marry the man whom she married, the man *whish-whish*ing downstairs. Peach? Orange? The man whose teeth are white and straight, except the gold tooth back deep, paid for by his years as Prudential's top citywide insurance man. Life, she remembers. He'd sold Life. Almost something she would laugh at, if her chest would rise.

He's … something … in the kitchen now, having left the middle room. Something with a bowl and a spoon. The clink of his cufflinks. The elastic snap of the rubber bands he wears to shorten his shirt sleeves. A chair groaning when he sits, and now he sits. Once she'd made the spaghetti and the sauce the way he'd liked it, had traded her Irish for his Italian. Once she'd never learned to bake a cake, just that steep of pie, Sarah's pie, she remembers now. Sarah, her sister. Harry, her brother, blowing the pie to cool with the cigarettes on his breath.

Harry, she thinks. *Harry*. My brother.

And then, again, the words of Emerson: *The world rolls; the circumstances vary every hour.*

Before she'd married she was the other version of herself, the one with the future she had planned. Before she'd married she was one of so many Finleys in the one house on Twenty-third, with the seesaw table and the stoop for air, the well inside her Pilgrim sweater, the calico that she can't figure into time, and the gull overhead, still missing its feathers, if she could only find her sweater, if she could give the feathers back.

If she could only take it all back and be that girl again,

—in the middle of

Wool

—in the middle of

Worsteds

—in the middle of

War

—in the middle of

Love with the boy with the split between his teeth, and not one golden molar.

The rain coming back through the wind drums its fingers into the song,

Among my—

The boy. All these years she has kept the news of him from her husband. All these years she has never mentioned Lani. All these years, she has hardly allowed for Harry and Sarah, and who will ever know who she once was, who she once loved, if she dies with all her secrets?

If only she could tell the girl, who will be old herself when she begins to guess this story, shape it. When she will wonder turquoise or peach, Lani or cinnamon, Monday or Tuesday, as the rain falls on the other side of her own window, as she does the math and counts: fifty-three years between now and then. It's not that she can't remember the boy's name. It's that it hurts too much to name him. It's not that they misspell her name in the obituary. It's that it will take the granddaughter all this time to fix it.

Finley.

Finley.

Finley.

Samuel Thompson Finley.

Jennie Semple.

Her Irish parents' names, the Finleys being farmers and weavers of way-back old and across the sea, from where the gull blows in to drop its feather.

Sarah, their first child.

Then Richard.

Then George, then Harry, then Jennie, then Margaret, then Ernest, then two more, she being the sixth of them, also called Peggy, and the one who reads the Little Library books from the Whitman's Sampler boxes, the newspapers with the missing ink, the books she'd borrow from South Philadelphia High, the new school at Broad and Snyder, the part they built for girls.

At home, in the past, Peggy sits in the darkest morning hour or the empty afternoon, before the boy who might have been her future comes, though he is coming. At the kitchen table with its shorter and longer legs in a house crowded with arguments, ridiculous with laughter, censored by lamplight and whatever they weren't allowed that week, Peggy sits, she reads.

Every time Peggy leans into a page, the sentences pitch.

The kettle for tea sends up indoor clouds. Her sweater is damp with the steam, less and less emerald in the green. If she remembers this, she will have to remember all of it. There is so much now to reckon with, and so little time to reckon.

The boy. She pictures the boy. When she dies he will be alive in no one's mind.

If only the girl would come.

The rain is gone now. The dark is sliding down

the windowpanes

with its fingertips

and now (how did this happen?) she has returned to the end of things, to night at 6840 Guyer Avenue in the city's southwest. She has returned to herself, lying thin in her bed—her mind following the sounds through the door, down the hall, past the painting of the white-faced horse, into the spare room with the practical mirror where the man she married has slept across her sickness years.

The unsnapping of the elastic bands around his sleeves.

Past him, through the farthest wall, through the brick, across the alley, past the fence, the prick of seagull beaks on playground macadam, the feather hem of wings scuffing the orange metal rim of the basketball hoop, which has been bent by the banging of the balls.

She can hear no further. The city beyond her is so far beyond her. Not hearing the lights still on, in the row houses, south. Not hearing the mew of a child, or the last scrapes of an argument, or the tangle in bedsheets, or an Alka-Seltzer fizz.

There is quiet where her listening ends, an odd and tremulous infinite, and now across the macadam the listening ricochets back, above peck and scuffle, past the fence, across the alley, through the brick, into the room where her husband is now out of his shirtsleeves and settling, this man she married in her chiffon dress with a handkerchief hem and holding her own secrets, her dominion over him.

Was it peach, or was it orange?

His greased hair greased back, his white T-shirt a fluorescence, his breathing coming on slow and loud, as if sleep is not the thing before the end. She will stay awake for as long as living is. Won't be long now, won't be—

The sound of his sleep, a rhythm interrupted by his dreams. Dance halls, she thinks. He dreams the foxtrot.

When she opens her eyes it is dark. When she closes them: also.

Closes them.

Breathes.

There. Again. That sharp stropping in the lowest part of her chest, beneath the thin white gown in which she lies but does not sleep. The cancer, she thinks. Its metal teeth. She breathes and it bites. She breathes and she thinks that when she dies the cancer will die, the cancer will be nothing without her—useless, homeless, no teeth. She will at the end of her dying send the cancer into obliterated retreat, and now, again, she breathes, and this time the pain is a temperature, a winter sinking deep.

It's okay, it is okay.

She breathes, and time is slipping.

It is winter 1918. The first day of the year

being just sixteen degrees, and the coal already in rations. Heatless Mondays by order of Harry A. Garfield, Federal Fuel Administrator. God being preached not in the churches but in the homes of those with lumps of coal and organs built of bleating reeds. The grocers are open on Mondays, the cigar shops with the pool tables in the ashy back. The war offices, the dentists, the doctors, the telegraphers, and the telephoners, but not much else on Market and Chestnut Streets, not school, either, not on Mondays, in this winter that's blown in.

Get up, she thinks. Get up, and stomp your feet. She hears the sound of the spotted mules and the wagons out on Twenty-third and the silence in between. No Model Ts, no Chevrolet Ds, no Overland Model 90 Bs, no automobiles in the thick drifts of snow on the streets. She hears Harry upstairs whistling, wonders if it hurts his lips to make a song when the air is shattering. What song is it? Whose—?

Or is that—

It is the first of January and then there is snow, days of snow, undifferentiated whiteness, and now it is January 13th—snow and rain and sleet and a 60 mph gale-force wind that blows the hem of her skirt when she sits in the kitchen hoarding stove heat. The wind is inside, its metal teeth. The bluster rippling the kitchen curtains and the tablecloth and the pages of the recipes and the soft curls around her mother's face.

At the boarding house of Mrs. Mary Campbell a chimney has been tossed from its perch and has smashed through the roof and landed on the bed of the two Larkin brothers, who might have died but for the luck that they'd not been able to make their way home, through the weather, from work. On the river the thick skin of ice is rising and buckling as the loose water flows beneath. In Manayunk the factories are calling for extra hands to hoist their war goods up to the floors where the floods won't get in.

And now Pops in the kitchen, too, rubbing the steam from the lenses of his eyeglasses with the sleeve of his shirt, saying the news is that they're arresting men for stealing the wagons they would use for the coal they would steal, were there coal to steal, were the coal not stuck north and west in its anthracite fields.

Fuelless, Pops says. Fuelless families. A name for them now, read it in the paper that arrives four and five days late. Pops worrying about the strangers and Ma with the tips of her fingers the same color as the vein that beats on her right wrist and Harry upstairs wrecking his lips with a song, Harry home from Baldwin's after his double shift, and Jennie, Jennie: She doesn't know where Jennie is, the others, too many to remember now, to place within the construct of this story.

Sitting in the kitchen, hoarding the heat.

X

Someday someone will get the few known facts wrong, put an X where a Y should be when they write her story. Someday her granddaughter, trying to imagine back the past, will discover the mistake in an old newspaper and make the declaration: *Wrong*.

Which is to say that one day, the report on her will look like this:

D'Imperio

Oct. 30, 1969, of 6840 Guyer ave.,
MARGARET A. FINLEX, wife of
Daniel D'Imperio. Relatives and
friends may call Sun. Eve., KISH
FUNERAL HOME, 6506 Elmwood
ave. Services Mon., 1 P.M. Int. Mt.
Moriah Cem.

And it will stay like this for decades.

But not yet.

There is still time to fix the facts inside the runnels of her mind. Ease what remains, let it come. No more pause or stutter now.

The wind knocks itself out. The snow stops. The sky goes

blue, and another day is blue, and then another, and then the clouds come in, unbearable with their own weight. Peggy hears the sound of the mules pulling the wagons through the streets, the thick crunch of the snow beneath the hooves, and now there is something else beyond, something detectable in the soles of her feet, her heart. She finds her second sweater, and her third. She borrows Harry's hat, pulls Ma's one wool scarf from the drawer in the room where they dance, adjusts the laces on her second-hand Hirsch-Ullmans and opens the door.

"Peggy?" she hears her mother call.

"I'll be back, Ma."

"You'll catch the death of you."

Halfway down the street, high-topping the slick of the ruts that the wagon wheels made, Peggy turns and sees Ma, her arms tied tight together at her waist, her top-step boots fit into the boot prints that Peggy's boots just made. She waves her mother back inside, pulling the cuffs of all three sweaters over her hand to keep it warm. Ma blows her a worrying kiss. Peggy waits just one more beat and pivots back into the chill breeze. She ducks her head, straightens Harry's hat, stomps Twenty-third, north.

The neighbor girl, Hannah, is out on the street. She is licking at an icicle. Peggy laughs and the girl's white teeth gleam.

The rut ice sliding her forward. The fallen snow shucking itself off the row-house roofs, the windowsills. The long-caught drip of the icicles catching the sun or the sky, so that the shafts of vertical ice are sometimes the color of goldenrod and sometimes crystal blue. She steps aside each time a new mule goes by, tugging its weight. Hellos the drivers. Waits until the ruts are hers again, the middle of the street. Her cotton skirt so thin. Her three sweaters in a twist. Her mother's orange scarf around her neck, loose, and Harry's soft fedora so low on her brow and so warm she feels her forehead prickles.

The sharp stropping of winter in her chest is released. The boy with the split between his teeth is headed her way, coming toward her like something she might wish, but there he is, up ahead, with a spotted mule of his own—a brine-colored, brown-spotted mule. No wagon, just the mule. She stops and waits, her toes gone numb in her boots. Above the fog of the beast's breath, his hand reaches for hers. She is pulled into the seat of his saddle.

"Heard you coming," she says.

He laughs, a funny wheeze of a sound: In. Out. He clucks at the mule, his father's mule, stabled in the back of a neighbor's leather shop. Peggy's heard the mule stories before. How he creaks his teeth when he chews. How he brays at the sight of the moon. His name is Sam. His ears are stretching east and west, flat like the wings of a gull a few minutes after takeoff. He makes a 180-degree turn in the street, and she holds on tight, pushing Harry's fedora back on her head and settling in against the boy's heat. She cuffs both her hands with the triple sweaters and locks them low about the boy's slender waist.

When they talk, but they hardly talk, their words are steam.

North, past Catherine, Fitzwater, Bainbridge, South. Past Lombard, Pine, Spruce. Past Locust, past Walnut, Sansom, Chestnut, Market, Arch, Cherry, then west toward the banks of the Schuylkill. The snow is everywhere in drifts, on the roofs, on the sills, on the stoops, in the wagons that wheel past, white on the red brick and on the brownstones and in the stonecutter's yards, frost on the glass of the Beer and Ale, the furniture maker, the cabinet maker, the narrow stoops of the houses, Loan and Storage, Laundry, the docks, the wharves, and she closes her eyes. Her head against the worsted wool of the boy's coat, her breath warms his neck.

Opens her eyes.

The river before her now, its buckled surface ice knocking the banks, its underflow crackling. Behind them the boathouses are still as postcards, strangely pristine between the soot and jam of river industry that has been silenced by the snow. Sam heaves. The boy leans over the beast's crest and extends a hand to his muzzle. Carrots, she realizes, from a bag she had not seen. She hears the old yellow teeth of the mule creak, the juice in its saliva.

"Listen," the boy says.

She sits straight in the worn saddle. She fixes her mother's scarf. Just the two of them, there on the east bank, in the frigid fog. Just him and her but also Sam, and now there, from across the river, at Thirty-fourth and Girard, it is: the zoo in deep song. The cinnamon bears and the hyenas, the prairie dogs and the tigers, the birds with their clipped wings noising up through their cages—howls and hoots and screams, small tinkers, trills.

It all rushes in, as if carried by the wind. One animal begins and another answers. One bird quits. More flutter. The honk and the haw of it. The squawk and shrill. The wing flap and rustle, until she can see, in her mind's eye, the largest elephant of them all upright on its hind legs, taking command with the baton of its trunk like Leopold Stokowski at an Academy matinee. Then blowing its own horn. She sees the long necks of the giraffes swaying. The white heads of the bald eagles nodding. The S shapes of the snakes sizzling. She leans. She snatches Harry's hat from her head with her sweater-mittened hands and kisses the boy's cheek. The smooth, cold, freckled places.

"How did you know?" she asks.

The boy shrugs. He won't break the spell of it, of them, in their balcony seats, at an animal concert, where now the tiger bellows, and—

Closes her eyes—

And—

the calico, she thinks, the calico.

New to its own mew.

He had something to tell her. News.

This was January. Or this was February.

Or.

She will not, in this hour, remember the boy's news. She'll keep them both just where they are: on the cusp of the future that will not belong to them, and this, she knows now, is what silence is—the memory you refuse.

No sound

from down the hall.

Her husband is long past awake, his shirt sleeves snapped, his black socks gartered. He's a few houses down the street with his best shoes on, sharing cherry biscotti with Edna Clancy's mother. They're talking the history of Life and the Great Depression, when he'd bring chicken eggs or a fist of parsley home because that's all that his customers could pay. Or maybe he's not with Edna's mother at all, but alone on a bench in the park, feeding the oily headed pigeons yesterday's loaf of sesame bread and watching the kids net the ball. Each bounce of the ball a tock, the lonesomeness of dying.

For him, too, she thinks. His lonesomeness of her dying.

Talk to me, Peg, he'd said.

She wouldn't.

Tell me where your thoughts go.

No. The thoughts were hers.

If the girl would come back, she would break her silence. If her father would find her where she is, by the creek, with the frogs, digging mica with the meat of her thumbs, and drive her in his green Dodge Dart from the suburbs to the city, the girl strapped into her mother's seat and the father singing his favorite sillies: *I've got tears in my ears from lying on my back in my bed while I cry over you.* If her father would park in the slant on the alley side so the girl could run—up the back stoop, through the galley kitchen, past the paintings, up the stairs. Her thick wool stockings with the creek dirt on each knee rumbling down her legs, pooling at her ankles, until, before she knocked, she would stop and yank the stockings up over her cotton underwear, fix the crotch sag, snap the elastic at her waist, done.

"Grandmom?"

And she would say, loud enough so the girl can hear,

"Betty—"

Making enough room in her bed for the girl to come and sit by her side and open her fist to prove the sparkle on her palm, her best found piece of mica. "Look," the girl would say. "It splatters." As if the rock had a sound to it. Her eyes would hurt for not seeing through the blur, and she would know again what she would still know when she was gone, about the girl confusing her own senses and being broken as a poem.

The girl would sit, she'd come to stay—her father reading the paper downstairs or watching Blackjack Lanza wrestling on the front-room TV, her husband and the girl's father side by side in the puffy parlor chairs, the father entertaining the wrestling out of pure, cool, professional, son-in-law courtesy. The girl would grow up to look just like her father, though when she'd become a writer with her age settled in, someone seeing a photo of her with her grandmother would claim a resemblance. *The eyes,* they would say. *The hair. You and your grandmother.* It would have been impossible for the girl to grow up to look just like her father and just like her mother's mother but she would never interfere with the deception, broken, as she would be, as a poem.

On the edge of the bed, the girl would sprawl, waiting for the start of the story before the end of the story, before the year that had changed everything. On the white sheets. In the fur-fuzz of the sun. She would reach for the girl's hand and the girl would put a hold on her ring finger, and then she'd pull the air up out of the battle of her lungs and begin.

Not at the start of 1918, but in March of 1917, which would be easier to remember out loud, at first.

Easier to yield.

Because if she began there, in 1917, she could pretend that Lani won't be dead. Or her mother. Or Harry. Or the boy. None of them could even be imagined dead, if she began her story in March 1917.

The Allies, she would say, were France, Britain, Italy, Japan, and Russia. The Centrals were Germany, Austria-Hungary, the Ottoman Empire, and Bulgaria. America was neither.

Breathe.

America was not at war. The President was a pacifist, saw no good in gore. Though the *Lusitania* had been sunk with Americans on board, and U.S. merchant ships kept going down, and food supplies weren't getting through, and the news was ugly all around. But in March 1917, America was not at war, and it was then, along the river's bank, that she had found the boy.

Listen, she would tell the girl. Listen. Come with me, return with me, to 1917.

It was the sound of the blue heron she'd been after—

its low-throated crick and the noisy cyclones of its paddling feet.

It was Jennie who'd claimed that a heron had come to that part of the river that wasn't sludge or sleaze, wharf or power—that stretch of trees and green by Boat House Row. Peggy had wanted to know for herself if it was true, the heron, or if it was plain mystification, and so she'd walked all that way, through the ramble of the city, her borrowed copy of *A Portrait of the Artist as a Young Man* slipped into her sweater pocket. It was Sunday. She'd carried the strange sounds of Joyce in her head as she went: *Once upon a time and a very good time it was there was a moocow coming down along the road and this moocow that was coming down along the road met a nicens little boy named baby tuckoo...*

A book to be memorized for the sounds it made.

And not forgotten.

Even now she won't forget it.

When Peggy got to that part of the river where the heron might have been, she stopped at the rock where she always stopped, arranged her things. The hem of the skirt about the edge of her boots. The pile of her sweater as a kind of cushion. There were, around her, others. Sunday strollers caught up in their talk. Kids managing their business. A kite. Some scullers. The face of the river was the sky it contained. No birds, then gusts of black birds. Then no birds again.

So she read.

He leaned his elbows on the table and shut and opened the flaps of his ears. Then he heard the noise of the refectory every time he opened the flaps of his ears. It made a roar like a train at night. And when he closed the flaps the roar was shut off like a train going into a tunnel.

The words felt smashed together. She liked the smash. She made a tent of the book across her lap and listened for the heron, hoped for a song from a long, feathered throat. Bird talk is music and music is pattern and pattern is color and she didn't know how long she'd been sitting here, the book balanced on her knee, her body hoping for the mystification of a heron, when she heard the curl of a song from down the way. A song sweet and high in its register, continuous except for when it took its breath, a call, a cry, a retreat, an advance. Not a heron.

She stood.

Breathe.

All along this stretch of the riverbank, there were rocks and roots and leaves. She walked. Her boots grew dark with end-of-winter mud. The low limbs of the near trees thwacked back and back as she passed. A river takes its own path. A river is never the same distance. She came closer and closer to the song she'd heard, which was the flare, she realized, of a brass bugle poked between the new spring leaves of a wide tree.

Bugle?

The song played on. The one stretch of the river that wasn't dying from anthracite slag and general garbage. When she reached the base of the tree and looked up, there he was. The bugle and the bugler. The song and the question. The boy.

She was Ma's well-mannered girl. She was School's Best at English. She was Harry's charm, Pops's favorite, Jennie's nag. No one to stop her from climbing that tree to the boy.

Tying her sweater around her waist, she fit her foot into the lowest notch of the trunk. Reaching for a higher branch, she found another notch, a knot, and climbed. A long sudden scratch on her arm beneath her pale blouse teased blood. Peggy was halfway up into the tree before the boy was close enough to reach his hand for hers. She felt the throb of the splinter in her thumb, that thin, long line of red on her arm. Jennie'd be mad. It was Jennie's blouse. She thought this, then forgot it.

Remembers it now. 1917.

"That's some pretty hardware," is what Peggy said, as she caught her breath. It was just the two of them on the thickest branch, in the new-leaf crown of the tree. This boy she'd see down at Twelfth and Market Streets when she was doing the shopping for Ma. He worked the stand on Saturdays, bagging the fiddleheads and pea greens, being gentle on the produce arriving from family farms west. He counted the money; he paid better attention than his brother or his Pa. He'd stand in the saw-dust, the trains rumbling overhead, the Market brats running in between the stalls but never knocking into him, and the first thing she'd noticed was how much he cared, and the second thing she'd noticed was how he dressed the part of an up-and-comer, and the third thing she'd noticed was how he carried a face that had goodness in it, but also something more, the glint of the future he was after.

The future *she* was after.

For a while that was all there was, her looking at him, him looking at her, and then one day, when she was checking a bulb of garlic for the fresh firmness of its cloves, he asked her her name. *Margaret, Peggy, Peg,* she said, and he chose Peggy. He had just one name, and she chose it, and after that they talked—the headlines, to begin with, and the weather, then other things that made her stop.

She wishes she could remember them now, what he had said that had carried her home, up Market and then over, south, until she was run-ning up her three stone steps, the fresh bulb of garlic in her pocket, calling out to Ma.

I met a boy.

Every Saturday morning: the shopping and the boy. Every Saturday so much to say, so many customers to stand aside for, so that they could continue talking. Until sometimes the entire week ahead of Saturday was Peggy collecting things to tell the boy, storing up wonders and oddments and protestations so that she could give them up and make them his, practicing turns of phrase she could hardly wait to exhale, because he liked her way of talking.

Living to tell how she lived. That's what it was. That's when it started.

Living to know what he would say, about the plans he was making, between the customers and coins, the bags, the Market brats stirring up sawdust.

All of that had been going by, weeks passing weeks, then months, and now it was Sunday and Peggy was up in a tree, by a river, the borrowed James Joyce in her pocket and a bugle held loose in his hand, a bugle catching the triangles of sun that filtered through the leaves.

She was face to face with the boy in a tree.

"So you're a bugler," she said. It wasn't something he'd ever told her.

"Not much to it," he said. "All you do is move your lips."

"Still," she said.

She smelled the brass on him, the market sawdust, the bark of the tree on the knees of his fine second-hand trousers. She leaned. He fit the bugle to her mouth and told her to blow and she did, and the thing squawked, scaring a poor pair of mallards off the river.

"Embouchure," he said, fitting his mouth to the mouthpiece and galloping the C the G the C. But still the ducks kept their distance and when he pressed the brass back to her lips and she tried again, he didn't laugh, but said: "If you don't think about it, it's easy."

She tried. It squawked. She surrendered.

"Who taught you?" she asked, returning the instrument.

"My pa," he said. "Who learned it from his. Family tradition."

Peggy tried to imagine the man in the fruit stall playing the bugle, but she didn't have enough imagination. He had a double chin and minor lips. His fingers were thick, seemed clumsy.

"Is this tree your rehearsal hall?" she asked.

"Tree doesn't seem to mind," he said.

"I was looking for a heron," she said, as if she was suddenly ashamed of having no greater purpose.

"The blue one?" he asked.

"You've seen it?"

"Heard it," he said. "Once. But never seen it. Saw you, though, down on the rock. Reading. Looked like you couldn't wait to turn the pages."

"James Joyce," Peggy said. "*A Portrait of the Artist as a Young Man*. It's a loaner. From my teacher."

She pulled the book from her sweater pocket. She started at the start: *Once upon a time and a very good time…*

Peggy stopped.

He was watching her face, saying nothing. She felt the throb of the splinter in her thumb, the heat in her face. She closed the book, but then he opened it again. "Go on," he said. "I could get used to it."

"Used to the story?" she said.

"Used to you reading the story."

She bit her lip. She worried the splinter.

"It will get dark," she said. "In no time."

He took her hand in his. He touched the splinter, began to ease it from her skin. A bright spurt of blood pooled. She watched the boy, his dark, wide eyes on the wound that pierced her skin.

"If you read more," he said, "I might start to understand it."

When

(she would tell the granddaughter)

she invited the boy home for the first time, in the month of May, and he arrived with a burlap full of asparagus that had just pushed its way up through the quiet part of the earth, and Ma said, "Will you look at that?" and she meant, *Will you look at him?*

When in June he arrived with a basket full of strawberries and every single one was a jewel, and when after that Ma put him to kitchen work for her, churning peaches into pie.

When, on Sunday afternoons in July, by the green part of the river, they watched the birds press the dots of their songs to the sky. The black and orange-breasted birds. The yellow-tummied birds. The caucuses of birds. The beaky sparrows. And she read to him on the rock that was hers. Joyce, again, still a book on borrow. And he didn't mind.

When, in the pale summer street dust, they would walk through the spill of antique shops on Pine Street—the Chippendale chairs out on the walk, the cast-iron settees, the weathervanes, the porcelain sinks, the frames without their pictures—or to Surprise Clothing or Twines & Thread or French Calf Skins or Freihofer Baking Company, taking as long as they wanted for their window shopping, or past B.F. Keith's at Chestnut and Eleventh Street, where maybe W.C. Fields would be appearing and they'd study his face on the poster, a pugilist's face, they would agree. When, at Rittenhouse Square, they'd sit with their scoops of Breyer's and spy the hover of a dragonfly pair or the stick of a praying mantis clinging to a shaft of vertical grass, and she called them lucky, and he didn't mind, his face full of the boast of it.

When the politicians and the bankers and the lawyers and the genteels and the proprietors flocked to the Jersey Shore—Cape May, Atlantic City, Beach Haven, Wildwood—and he and she were favoring the Automat of Horn & Hardart on Chestnut Street instead, each nickel a choice they'd spent the weeks before making, each dish in its own framed window (Salisbury steak or creamed spinach or liverwurst sandwich or pie), until they put their nickels in and the little doors released and whatever they'd wanted for weeks was theirs to eat, and each cup of French-style drip coffee arrived warm through the elegant snout of a metal dolphin, while outside, possibly, it was raining and the streets were puddling and the cars and the horses and the trolleys were thick with the mess of it, so they stayed inside, as long as they wished, the marble at Horn & Hardart like a luxury that fit.

And how they'd stand in the stained-glass shadows of the Broad Street Theater which was once Kiralfy's Alhambra Palace on the east side of South Broad—stand there, in September, across from the red-brick infamy of the Academy of Music when the Saturday matinees let out, hoping for a sighting of the great wild-haired conductor Leopold Stokowski and his wife Olga Samaroff and the great patrician Mr. Edward Bok and his wife Mary Louise Curtis. Standing there just to get a sight of them—he for the clothes they'd wear and she for the styles of their hair—and then hum what they each knew of Mahler or then of Brahms on the way back to South Twenty-third, though she knew "Pretty Baby" better, and "I Love a Piano," and "Turn Back the Universe and Give Me Yesterday," so that halfway there, her arm tucked through his, she'd sing those other songs, and shim-sham her hips, and he would never mind, and when, after they turned the corner onto Peggy's block, there Hannah was, her smile a gleam, dipping her chin in rhythm with the song.

Shhh.

All of this she will tell her granddaughter when her father brings her. She will name the good days by their ways. Give them to the girl so that the cancer cannot win.

She will die, she will accept her dying, if her remembering lives.

Not 1918 rushing 1917. Not the President giving his wartime speech. Not the Senators and the Representatives voting Yes. Not the wildly charitable proposition of the Liberty Loan Act. Not the Selective Service Act, men the ages of 21 through 30 to start with, until they would need more men, more women.

What she loved was taken from her. Stolen. She will steal it all back.

In the last days

of the year that is 1917, the boy with the space between his teeth is nineteen. He has a future that teems. He is a scholarship student at Philadelphia Textile, in the Greek gleam of the building at Broad and Pine. In Wool. In Worsteds, the better yarn from the better sheep and the smarter carding. "You should see the machines," he says. He'd been acclaimed to his spot by the principal at South Philadelphia High, the boys' part, and approved by the Board of Education, and that is how he'd gotten in, for free, that and his enthusiasm, the way he studied things.

He likes knowing the numbers and repeating them. He likes telling Peggy wool stories in between what she reads to him. Sometimes her brother Harry will laugh at the boy's obsession behind his puff of smoke, or her sister Sarah will shake the Irish curls on her head, passing the two of them on the stoop. "Wool again," she'll say, tsking. "Wool talk."

Which sets the cat across the street to mew and Lani to opining.

But Peggy listens. Peggy commits every fact the boy delivers to the beats of her own heart: Seven hundred thirty-six spinning, weaving, and knitting establishments in her city. One hundred dyeing and finishing works. One hundred twenty-eight raw-wool dealers. Eighty chemical and dyestuff firms. The numbers there in the boy and laid out in the pages of his school catalog, which he brings to her so she can read it out loud, into the nights that keep falling. Proof, he'll say, as she pores over the pretty print until it can't be seen in the chill dark, that he is truth-telling. As if she ever doubted him.

Love isn't hard. Love is hard. Love might have been just this.

At the big building with the big windows, he is training to fit in, growing his expertise, as he likes to say, words as fancy as the new bowler he'll buy one day, when he is rich, when they are. He makes a list of all he learns: Grades of wool from various breeds of sheep. Cause of shrinkage. Pulled wools. Burring and picking. Theory of carding. The principles of grinding. Hand, ball, creel, condensers, single and double doffers, steel blade dividers.

Practicing to borrow off of the man he'll be, when he gets his degree, when he is someone in Worsteds, the finest yarn there is, from the finest sheep.

Already he can afford to buy Peggy her Whitman's, the Sampler boxes with the luxury little books tucked in.

There is a price of textiles. The price that her city pays for being the Workshop of the World. The expense is the boys and the girls who'd lost their fingers and their wrists, smashed their feet, inhaled the poison fumes of dyes, worked the day shifts and the moon nights in the mills of Kensington and Manayunk. Mother Jones and her March of the Mill Workers is a true story. The stink in the river, the unpleasant wafts on the breeze: True. The textile amputees stealing coal from the coal yards down on Washington Street, one piece of the black brick at a time: True.

Textile workers. Wools. And Worsteds.

But down at Twenty-sixth and Reed, a family of proprietor-philanthropists named Fleisher is raising up from crumpled ground a brand-new building, the largest yarn and braid factory in the world—a consolidating enterprise in the company's fiftieth year. Peggy has watched the building grow. She has stood a safe distance from the spectacle beside the boy as the concrete has been poured, the bars put up, the red brick and the light brick layered in, tasteful and ornamental.

Construction drifts block the streets on some days. Scaffolding steps the men up high. The buildings take shape with their indents and rises, driveways and heights, near the steel hunger of the rail lines. The dyehouse fronts Dickinson. The powerhouse possesses its own patch of rumbled ground. The Ionic columns rise on either side of the main entrance at Reed. The ribbed-glass sectionals, going in near to last, promise interior daylight—

and the two of them standing there, Peggy's arm looped through his, a stray dog sniffing at their feet, the wind catching their hems. There's the hard graze of the construction dust in their eyes, and so they blink. Peggy is aware of her height, her inches above him, thanks to the elevating heel in her sturdy Hirsch-Ullmans and to genetics. She is aware, too, of how she bends toward him, how attentively she listens for the words blowing through the gap between his teeth, the words explaining the news of the building. Passenger elevators. Comfort arrangements. Locker rooms. A hospital. A recreation room. Sprinklers. Steel doors. Rolling sashes. Conveyor systems. An employee dining room on the sixth floor, where the managers would work. The wool sorting on the fifth floor. Carding, combing, spinning on the fourth and third floors. Shipping on the second floor. Washers and driers on the first floor. Dyeing in the dyehouse. The storage of dangerous and extra things in the basement.

"Look," he'd say.

"One day," he'd say.

He'd run the Worsteds at Fleisher's.

Loudly, in the thick of noise, he'd speak. The boys in the Navy Yard not far down the street.

Both of them carrying on with their eternal imaginations.

Selectee

It sounded better. *Selectee*. As if you had won or had become the next thing more supreme than elite. *Selectee*, and soon you'd be on a train to Camp Meade—your tweed cap on, your smooth leather bag thick with what you'd think you'd need, your jacket worsted, your eyes turned back to what you were leaving, who.

Standing on the platform.

Short, dark, wavy hair,

and tall,

and pretty.

Who.

News, you'd said. *I have news.* That's the way you put it. When the chimpanzees were playing their drums and the elephants were hoof and sway and the birds were doing all the work of the sopranos.

And she'd said *no, no*, kept saying *no*. Slapping you across the face, saying *no*. One single slap made harsher with the cold, and with the way she looked, like you could break her, like you'd already broken her, and you couldn't hear the singing anymore.

Onto the 40 x 8. Taking your place in the rumble with the Russians, the Poles, the Hungarians, the Greeks, the Serbs and the Slavs, the Italians, hardly finding your own language in the talk on the train over the rails to Odenton, to Camp Meade, which had been nothing but fruit trees and corn silks until July 1917, and which was bigger than a city now, a timber city, wind blowing through the planks in the walls and some of the roofs overhead still mere two-by-fours pounded together into peaks, as if that were any shelter from the winter, which was cold.

At Camp you'd have six inches, if luck was with you, between your cot and the adjacent selectee. His breath on your face. His dreams in whatever language he dreamed in. The extra length of his newspaper when he fell asleep. Old fly paper and old stuck flies and your mess kit above his mess kit—all those mess kits on all those wooden trays banged into all those barrack posts.

Yes, Sir, Major General Joseph Kuhn. Yes, Sir, Lieutenant. Yes Sir, Major. Yes, Sir, and suddenly you'd be getting by with half your name in a place crammed with men like you, except you couldn't understand most of what some of them said and none of your stories were the same, and she was the only one like her, still standing on the platform, planted there, hands in her Pilgrim sweater pocket, emerald green, wind in her hair, her brother beside her, Harry, his arm across her shoulders.

"Don't let her come alone," you had made him promise, and he'd said, "I'll be there, I'm coming."

"I'll be back," you told her mother. Stood there in that kitchen, making declarations, while the girl sat in the other room, her face full of the puff of its sadness.

You gave your bugle to the girl. You told her it was easy, just blow it and that's practice. You said that when you got back from war you'd be expecting a concert.

Embouchure, you said.

She wouldn't believe you. She blamed the President and the Congress. She blamed the U-boats and the Kaiser. She blamed the man with the gun who'd killed the Archduke. She blamed the other men who could not go to the war that he'd be fighting except she didn't blame Harry, who couldn't go due to his weak heart, and she didn't blame Pops, who was too old now to march, and because she would never, in her anger, blame them.

"You come back," she said, "and I'll stop blaming."

The trenches would be mud—twelve feet you'd dig in zig-zag configurations. The afternoon drills would be up and over the chunks of interference you'd hammer together in the morning. The rifles would be dummies, then the John M. Brownings and then the M1917 machine guns and then the fabric ribbons of ammunition belts and then the Chauchat light machine gun, the special care and feeding of which would be reported on directly by the French themselves, wearing their fine cylindrical hats and their remarkably wide coat pockets.

I do not blame you but I cannot save you and it's coming. I wind back the clock, reset the days, but it's coming. Too young for the first draft, you were right-aged for the second. You were called and you had had no choice but to head to the city's center and stand in that office before the banker and the lawyer and the fire chief who were deciding. There was no hiding. They'd said, *Next, Next, Next* to the men who came before you—the men hollowed by rickets or stooped by factory work or limp in one foot thanks to a machining. They'd said *Next,* and then there you were—whole and young, a college boy on scholarship, complying with the rules. Your name plain and clear and uncomplaining on the registration card. You had a future in worsteds. They said *Yes* to you.

I wind back the clock, but I can't save you.

The days that remained were winter. By the end of February you'd be bound for Meade, a camp named after a general you had read about in school.

A doughboy now. Destroy the Kaiser.

She blamed, most of all, the Kaiser.

I write you the split between your teeth. I write you the hand you lift to say goodbye, the book you wish to barracks-read at night, in the light of the moon, within the shadow of the big clock outside that reads the size of the Liberty Loans instead of time—your novel, your history, your poem: *The Pennsylvania Museum and School of Industry, Circular of the Philadelphia Textile School, Broad and Pine Streets.*

The broad and thorough educational policy steadfastly adhered to by those who shape the School's character, has resulted in the graduation of a body of young men who by reason of the breadth of their training have been enabled to enter all fields of the work, and to-day they are well and favorably known in every textile section of any importance. They are in the mill, the dye-house, the commission house, and the machine builders, and wherever found they are proving themselves capable men and an honor to their alma mater.

I write you as sure as I have ever been.

I do not wish to harm you.

It's cold in February.

It's worse in March. Peggy wraps herself in sweaters and sits on the stoop to read, Lani nattering across the street above her: *You'll catch your death of—*

When Peggy walks she walks south and west. She walks to Fleisher's, stories tall at Twenty-sixth and Reed. Stands at the corner, imagining. So many divots of fresh sun cut in, a lustrous window glaze, a considerate decline to the dyeing-room floor, and the boy with the air between his teeth gone to the Great one.

When she sits she reads the news on the stoop. The war as told through headlines. The home-front life in the classifieds.

4 Philadelphians Escape as U-Boat Torpedoes Tanker

29 Lost, 10 Saved When Patrol Tug Sinks Off Capes—Operator Sticks to Post—Lieut. Edward D. Newall, 23-Year-Old Commander, Believed Among Those Lost—Leaves Young Wife Here—Other Philadelphians on the Ill-Fated Vessel

American Forces on Line of Battle Increase Rapidly—Speeding Up Process Taken to Mean Extension of U.S. Sector—Newer Divisions Will Go to Front as Fast as They Are Trained

U.S. Soldiers Fighting with Rifles and Pistols

Girls for Shipping.

Girls for Spinning.

Girls for Dyeing.

She'd wonder who'd write such a thing and not decide to change the wording later.

Remembering rages because

the story grows specific.

Hannah, that neighbor girl with the black hair. Where is she now?
Would she remember?

Contested Information

"(T)he largest yarn and braid factory in the world has been taken over by the Federal Government and will be devoted exclusively to the manufacture of war goods... The plant, like Ford's, will become an integral part of the Philadelphia depot of the Quartermaster's Corps, and will be devoted to the manufacture of army uniforms."

A characterization later contested: "The urgent needs of the Government for modern manufacturing space, however, prompted Messrs. Fleisher to offer a part of the new mill to the Quartermaster's Department. This offer has been accepted."

More and more,

Peggy sees what it is: The city is yarn. Uncountable miles of doughboy khaki and the clack of gauged metal needles. The sound of the yarn is on the stoops, on the other side of open windows, on the street corners where women stand, the hanks of it in their baskets, their hands moving fast beneath their aggravated worry.

You can help, the American Red Cross posters promise, and who doesn't want to send the soldiers more to wear than the overcoat and stockings the U.S. Corps floats them into battle with, into places she doesn't want to imagine.

The rumor is soon. Soon the Boys' Brigade will be on the move—from the south to the north, on the rails to a harbor, among a crowd on a ship on the seas. Soon he will be reading about worsteds by the lamp of the moon, waiting for battle in trench smoke mist, counting the bullet holes in trees, the near misses of war. Soon. And all this while the women of her city knit, Jennie knits, sometimes Ma—sweater vests and socks, balaclavas, trigger-fingered mittens. All this while they obey *The Delineator*, its exhortations and instructions:

In war more men die from cold and exposure and illness than from wounds. Every hour that you waste, you are throwing away the life of one of your soldiers. Do you dare shirk? Set aside a part of each day for your war work. It may tire you a little. What of it? Do you think our Army is ignorant of fatigue? It may mean the occasional sacrifice of a luncheon, a tango tea or a theater party. And if it does? Our men are giving up every pleasure, every comfort, every home tie; offering up their bodies and their lives.

Directions for Sleeveless Sweater

3 hanks of yarn (3/4 lb.)

1 pair Red Cross needles No. 3

Cast on 80 stitches.

Knit 2, purl 2 stitches for 4 inches.

Knit plain until sweater measures 25 inches.

Knit 28 stitches, bind off 24 stitches for neck, loose.

Knit 28 stitches.

Knit 5 ridges on each shoulder, cast on 24 stitches.

Knit plain for 21 inches. Purl 2, knit 2 stitches for 4 inches.

Sew up sides, leaving 9 inches for armholes.

2 rows single crochet around neck and 1 row single crochet around armholes.

Completed articles should be turned in to the Red Cross through the nearest Chapter or, when not convenient, mailed direct to any of the places given on page 71.

The wings of the airplanes inside the skies of war are outfitted with linen; spare the linen. The doughboys are dying of cold in the trenches; yarn them scarves and socks and trigger-fingers. There are men walking their European streets in suits made out of paper. There are ladies strutting silks in daylight hours. There are hems going up, jackets gone sleeveless; there is everyone doing their part. Whatever can be done with less, do for less. Whatever sacrifice might be made in the name of cotton, wool, and linen, make it. Find your needles, bruise your fingers, mute the pounding of your heart with the clack,

the clack

of the knitting as Peggy walks. The sound of the women on the stoops, on the corners, in the parks, saving the ones they love with yarn, the sons, the husbands, the brothers, the boys. The million-mile miles of wooly and wild, as if the yarn streamers behind as she walks, as if she were the Grand Marshal of the war-effort parade, as if the boy with the space between his teeth will be coming toward her, running toward her, if she just walks far enough.

Girls for spinning. Girls for dyeing. Girls for balling. Anyone can ball.

Lani is doing her war part at Whitman's. She's twenty-eight years old, no husband in sight, no husband wanted. She comes home smelling crystalline and sits in her pale-blue slip in her second-story window telling stories about the candies she helps make, the millions of tins being sent to the boys who will fight and win the war. The sash pushed up, the curtains rippling, doesn't matter the weather, she talks. She talks the hats and aprons that the candy ladies wear. She talks the stiff wood chairs and the long tables, how the best part of the whole place is the light that comes in from the lengths of the city. She talks the white-brick room where the men too old for war crack and shave the coconuts, then save the shells for the government—ship them off to Edgewood Chemical Biological Center at Aberdeen, where they are set on fire and reduced to powdered charcoal, which has miraculous powers of gaseous absorption, she says, which is needed (but she can't explain just how) to save the boys in their gas masks.

At least that's how Lani talks it, from her second-story perch, the one strap of her slip looping down and off her shoulder. Sweets with a book. Sweets in the trenches. Sweets beneath the moon.

Lani can't surpass the ingenuity of it all, the way everything has its purpose. Lani can't imagine that any more could be done for the boys across the sea, who have gloves now, and chocolates, books, and masks. He'll be fine, she tells Peggy. He'll be fine. About the boy. Whose last letter arrived three weeks ago, nothing since. But Lani doesn't read the news that is thumped from house to house, down Twenty-third. She doesn't bother with the *Inquirer* and its headlines, its vulgar cartoons, the torpedoes, the impetuous, the dead. Lani doesn't read the news, why read the news, for what more can Lani do but cover the coconut-cream centers with the luscious milk chocolate, and encourage the coconut crackers?

Two months ago, Lani was packing the chocolates into the Whitman's Samplers, working each piece like she might work a puzzle, one chocolate beside the other in its box.

Now Lani sits in another room on a stool with the white hat on, the white apron, passing coconut centers through the coating machine, a job which, she says, requires rhythm, a job at which she's superior. The talk over the machines. The misshapen creams the workers eat. Lani's teeth tasting like sweets. One of the men who cracks the coconuts sometimes walks Lani all the way home, from the factory at Fourth and Race, to her house on the other side of South Twenty-third. Gives her a kiss on the cheek, his stubble roughing up the kiss side of Lani's face. Lani's mother, Mrs. Sperr, watches from inside with her rheumy eyes and tsks. The women of the street look up from their knitting needles, their—

miles and miles of—

and do not speak their condemnation loud enough for Lani to hear, though Peggy does. Peggy hears what the neighbors think, how they assume that the German in Lani is to blame for her ways, how they call her Kraut when she can't hear, how they question her affinities.

The sounds of things like the breath of things, the sigh going in, going out, going down, going up, yarn for miles, like streamers.

October—but what day?—1969

There's moon tonight. The rain has stopped. The girl has been gone now for days. When she is older, so much older, the girl will want to tell this story of her grandmother, will want to put it down in words, and when she cannot find the story, when she is old herself, she will pull all her paints from the shelves, all her tools from the drawers, all the salts and glues and dried leaves and severed phrases she's been storing, the few spare photographs left to her in a Bloomingdale's box, the sheets of music scoured off the internet, and make what she can.

An amateur artist dissatisfied with words.

Art instead of story. Becoming, then, the story.

Come back, she wants to tell the girl. *Come back so I can tell you.*

Shim-Me-Sha-Wabble is the name of the song in

the brick house they'd painted red. Three bedrooms for the flock of them back when none of them were dead. The *exquisite equipoise*, she likes the sound of that, like something she'd have found in one of those little books, had she —

If the girl would come back, she would give her the pearl. She would stand up, shake out her bones, feel the scant weight of herself on her two bare feet, and cut across the room toward the dresser (three steps, four) and pull open the drawer and snap open the lid of the box, in which there are two nested boxes. In one of the boxes is the pearl. In the other is the hat pin that will be stolen by the dance-hall woman her husband will marry soon after she's gone.

How many years? It doesn't matter. Too soon.

She would give the girl the pearl, and she would say: *Take what is yours, do not forsake it.*

But the girl has been driven away in her father's green Dodge Dart, its windows down, the city blurring to a nub behind her. The girl has gone to her house with a yard, a strawberry patch, a fallen bird in the strawberry patch, a new swing set with a faulty chain that will someday crack and send the girl to breaking in many ways and places. But not yet. The girl lives on Maple Shade Lane in a neighborhood muddy with a spare creek and fluffy with kittens that hatch in secret places beneath the neighbors' porches.

The girl has that cat of her own, that found calico named Colors, just like the girl to name her found cat Colors. Sometimes the girl leaves the fresh-hatched kittens and the fallen bird and the thicket patch of strawberries and her own cat behind and, in her best dress up—patent leather shoes, patent leather purse, white straw hat—she is packed into the Dart with her father and mother and brother and sister and zoomed to the Hotel DuPont for Sunday brunch, where some women eat with white gloves on and the ceiling is so high above them the girl believes it is an extension of sky, the gold part of the sky, or heaven, maybe, from where the angels watch, waiting for their seat at the table. Angels eating French toast. Angels eating berries. So she imagines, for the girl.

Or—

Wearing the pair of culottes her mother Singer-sewed, the girl is sped along, all the glass in the car rolled down, to a shack they call The Charcoal Pit, where they serve ice-cream cones on plates, the ice-cream part face down and the cones pointing up like hats. Smoke above the Pit. Chocolate candies for the ice-cream eyes and one single chocolate circle for the ice-cream nose. The girl worries every time about whether she should eat the face of the ice cream, ruin the pointy crusty hat. Poor ice cream, losing its hat, losing its face.

Betty—

Boop—

A girl to be taken seriously.

What time of night, or has the day come on?

She closes her eyes, and it's the parlor she sees,

and —

Harry and her mother and the girl she was,

dancing. It's scandalous, Peggy's mother says, behind her smile, the way Peggy sinks to the moan of the jazz saxophone. The way Peggy cat steps, turkey trots, camel walks, shivers her shoulders when they put the needle down on Shim-Me-Sha-Wabble.

Peggy stubs the songs out with the round parts of her heels and the Victrola hangs on, doesn't fall, despite all the bounce in the room.

Scandalous, a sibilant word. Throwing all her lonesome at the shaft beneath the song.

Her brother and her mother clear the parlor when Peggy's dancing. They put the fragile things where they cannot fall. They stand beneath the arch that separates the parlor from the kitchen, and there, on the fringes, they dance, working the songs out with modesty and pleasure. Peggy's mother takes the lead. Harry follows, his hand on his heart. Whoever is upstairs calls down the stairs for quiet, leans across the banister in their house tunic and hair pins.

"Peggy, could you please?"

"Peggy, do you have to?"

Peggy blames them back.

"Have a little fun, will you?"

Making a sweet nugget of a false case for pretending that the boy's not gone. That Woodrow Wilson had no Fourteen Points and no Four Principles either, and that the Brits were not dying in the Battle of Picardy, or fighting for their lives in Armentières and also, by the way and while she's at it, that Lt. Douglas Campbell had never had any good or righteous cause to shoot the German fliers down.

Peggy's mother is out of breath. Harry can't contain his. Holds the cigarette above his head as he makes his moderate moves. When her mother steps into the longest beam of window sun, Peggy—grinding and shagging and sliding like the song tells her to—stops and sees the soft down on her mother's face, the blue vein in her neck, the translucent spill of something on the left sleeve of her frock, the way she was young once, not a woman managing many in a house rightly built for four and a kingdom of things tucked into one trunk of treasures brought on her wedding day to Samuel Thompson Finley, a separate century ahead of this one. Which includes lace from the home country, Ireland. Which includes a doorknob from her own mother's front door. Which includes a gold bracelet with a droplet of pearl.

Which includes—well, there are things even Peggy can't know. Even the granddaughter, now imagining.

Harry sees what Peggy sees, through the wisping smoke of his lit cigarette. He sees their mother, and that is why Harry is Peggy's favorite brother, why what will happen must not happen, must be kept in the dark from the truth, because Harry loves their mother best.

Harry plants a kiss on her cheek before he leaves each day for Baldwin Locomotive Works, where they were, for a time, building Péchot-Bourdon locomotives for the French trench railways, but where now they are making machines for the doughboys—Baldwin 2-6-2 steam locomotives, 60 cm gauge. Harry is not on the front and the war needs him here, gauges and cylinders and steam pressures. Peggy can't quite find the logic in the way the locomotives come to be, out of paper, into metal, out of a factory onto a ship, how the locomotive tonnage does not sink the ships to the bottom of the seas, how anything or anyone is saved from the bottom of the sea.

U-Boat Torpedoes Tanker

What Peggy knows is that Harry works more with a pencil than a pair of pliers or a hammer or whatever they use to build the trains for the war. Harry works with his head, their mother says, watching him off, down the stoop, down South Twenty-third, in the early part of the day.

"You and Harry," her mother says, standing in the door, Peggy just behind her. "You and Harry and your heads."

It's Pops she hears coming down the stairs

and into the parlor where the dancing is and toward the patch of sun spilled on the floor by the open door. Pops who is planting his kiss on her mother's lips, tucking a loose silvering curl behind her mother's ear, then walking the three stoop steps backwards before he turns and heads off to the Arsenal to pound the soles onto the boots the soldiers need, you can't knit the boys into boots.

April 1918. A Daylight Saving's hour. Harry and Ma and Peggy, dancing.

Pops leaving, dressed smart in his work waistcoat, his trousers creased, the gold-rimmed spectacles he pushes back up the thin bridge of his nose with the bent outer part of his wrist. Pops down the street, and her mother blowing him a kiss that he can't see, maybe feels. Pops gone.

"Pansies have their faces on," Peggy says, looking across the street at the window box Lani's mother has hung and planted, their part of the war effort, Lani had explained, two nights before, their part of being more American than German, making things nice for Philadelphia, Workshop of the World, arsenal giant, men and women going to work and needing a little beauty in their passing.

"And the sun is full," Peggy's mother says, waving to Hannah as she skips her way by. "Full as the moon last night, did you see it, Peggy?"

Peggy says yes. Says she had left Jennie's side in the bed the sisters share, Jennie whistling as she slept, a high note coming through her nose. Down the stairs into the living room and then through the house she'd come to sit on the stoop to watch the moon lift itself up, or surrender itself to being lifted. Doesn't confide the other part—how she had sat there thinking that the boy in his training camp might be watching it, too, might be reading by the lamp of it, his catalogue on worsteds, her letters, six of them now, best as she could write them.

News of the house, she has written. News of the street, of school, which hardly actually concerns her, some of the teachers gone to war or factory jobs, some of the students, too, everything in fractions. News, too, of the goings-on at Fleisher's, which she watches from the corner of Twenty-sixth and Reed, the people coming in and out, the smokestack smoking. She has tried to describe, in her letters to the boy, the sound of the yarn in the city, the way the yarn streamers after her when she walks, the way the city can't be yarn without him.

She is reading Emerson, she has written to confess, to find the words.

The passion re-builds the world for the youth. It makes all things alive and significant. Nature grows conscious. Every bird on the boughs of the tree sings now to his heart and soul. The notes are almost articulate.

Her heart, she thinks. *Her* soul.

Remembering the sound of the animals singing.

Saturday. Laundry day.

Upstairs Peggy's older sister Jennie and her younger brother Ernest are stripping the sheets from the beds, because the order on laundry day is lights first, then darks, the things with stains that can't be sponged off bundled up and carried down the splintered wooden steps into the basement, where the Triumph Rotary Washer does its triumphant work.

It's Peggy's turn to operate the machine, but she won't today, she's suddenly free of the drudge of it, the sloppy suds, the stirring stick, because Pops has left for work without his silver pail and its slice of yesterday's vegetable pie, the apple they'd put on reserve for him, tart and out of season, but still the fruit that Pops prefers, something set aside by the boy's father when she visited the stand last week, when they talked, above the crowd, of the boy and his letters. Pops has left his pail shining bright on the kitchen table, like he sometimes does, in the absent-minded hours of his double-shifting mornings.

"Ma," Peggy calls up the stairs to explain, and before her brother or her sister can stop her, she's back out into the sun, slamming the front door behind her, jumping the stoop, running all the way to the Schuylkill Arsenal in her high-tops, her sweater flapping behind her, two feathers in her pocket. The guards let her pass. They always do. They understand that her business here is bringing a hard-working man his lunch in a pail.

Through and in, she stops. Catches her breath. Stands before the latitudes and longitudes of chalkers and cutters and sewers and tappers and pounders and finishers. Reels inside the crushing noise of it. Until someone passing points her toward where the cobblers work, and she walks, slow and steady now, down and down the row of warfare work, until she sees a man, mostly older than the rest, adjusting the wire frames on his nose with the bent back of his wrist. Until she is close enough for him to feel her shadow fall against him.

"Pops?" she says.

He turns. Stops the machinery of his work, the rhythm of it, while every man on either side pounds and pounds and pounds. Latitudes. Longitudes. Her father, his face flush with the heat of his exertion, her own face doubling back at her inside the lenses of his glasses, the noise too over-shattering for either of them to try to speak. She leaves the pail on the floor by his feet. He says her name, but she can't hear it. She wonders how, at night, Pops hears anything but this, the terrible thunder of the Arsenal, the everlasting echo.

Peggy leaves the way she came, up the endless row of hunch and hands and cobbling. She salutes the guards and they salute her back and she reappears inside her city.

She stops to let a wagon pass, a woman with two sticks of bread torpedoing out from the clench of one arm, a mutt with a sock in its mouth, a girl her age carrying a single daffodil like she's practicing for the wedding aisle. She walks home, doesn't run, lets the hour exhaust itself, this Saturday in April.

Let Ernest run the lights. Let Ernest. Let Jennie. All morning long her thoughts will be beaten into nothing by the thunder of the Arsenal. She will see herself, doubled, in the eyesight of her father, versions of herself that do not speak for herself to anyone who can listen. The sentence running long, and short.

"What took you so long?" Jennie is saying now, at the bottom of the basement steps, where the Triumph waits. The darks.

Peggy takes a good look at Jennie, her prettiest sister who can wear any rags at all, any hand-me-down or out-of-season fashion and still look all dressed up, thanks to the color of her eyes. She says her best *I'm sorry*.

Easter

is better than Christmas. Pansies not snow, her best shoes, her soft sweater, and the baskets the—

opens her eyes—

the only day she ever forgot that she was dying. Easter. Of the Resurrection. Of Christ rising. When she could slip the gut twist of the cancer from her thoughts, how many years had it been since the cancer had been birthed in the dark of her stomach and metastasized, diabolical, like some terrible sea monster. The cancer—

the.

She'd get the whole affair of the baskets started weeks in advance, forecasting Easter, leaving Christmas to Christmas, Valentine's Day to the red construction-paper hearts Scotch taped to the glass porch-windows, faded now. Easter being hers because it is held in her own house, and not near the creek on Maple Shade Lane.

6840 Guyer Avenue. Her house. With the alley in the back and the bounce of the balls just past the alley, in the park, and the ham with the pineapple slices in the oven, and too many plates, but everyone fits around the dining-room table. Her china. Silverware she'd polished.

There is a shop at Fifty-second and Market—stationery, trinkets, sour balls, party pleasures, Whitman's Samplers, in honor of Lani. It is her shop and her son's shop, her beautiful, tall, and dark-haired son, who makes things with his hands—Christmas ornaments, Valentine's Day cards, Easter dioramas in the shape of crystal eggs, place your eye to the peephole and find Alice in her Wonderland or a bunny in a garden— they sell it all at the shop. The two of them. Mother and son, though it's hard for her to get there now, to stand there all day, not to crumple from the pain of her greedy disease, but she does, she tries. Like somebody writing a book, she wrote the shop.

When Easter is coming she buys from herself at wholesale prices—bamboo baskets with long-looped handles, pink in the weave, and green, and blue, baskets chosen according to the personalities of her three grandchildren. Bamboo baskets and Easter grass. Jellybeans sprinkled like sugar seeds. A coconut cream and a pretty hollow and an egg-shaped diorama through which entire worlds can be seen. Sequined and tasseled. Paper gardens. Girls. One diorama each. Getting ready for Easter.

And then the crinkle of ribbon tied to the base of each basket handle, miles and miles, she thinks, miles and—

one long ribbon to each basket, each leading to treasure. Miles that, upon her personal word, the girl and her brother and sister will chase until the ribbons come to their hysterical ends beneath the sofa or up the stairs or wherever she had run them, one ribbon per child, three ribbons. At the end of the ribbons, there are her best-made plans—a book for the girl, a doll for the sister, a puzzle for the boy who likes numbers. The hoopla of Easter. The squeals that come from the kids when the ribbons length themselves out and the gift is there at the end of the line, the kids going fishing in her house.

Over too soon. March. Sometimes April. The gifts run all the way back to her, *Look, Grandmom, Look.* The girl stepping up on the little lacquered step stool that has been placed there for just this purpose, a stool that gives the girl more height beside her own upholstered rocker. So that the girl might plant a kiss on her grandmother's cheek. She is already so weak. She hopes nobody sees. She is pale against the pastel brights of Easter, beside the lacquer. The girl stands on her step stool, precipitous, her thick wool stockings bunching up around her ankles and her bangs cut at a terrible angle. She stomps and the stockings bunch even more grandiosely. At the top of her stool the girl kisses her grandmother's cheek again. A whisper. A tickle. A giggle.

Freckles, too.

Jellybean breath.

Chiclet teeth.

Thank you, Grandmom. I love you, Grandmom. The girl says, clamboring down now, from her stool. The girl putting her stick arms out and starting to spin, or is she dancing, it's hard to tell with that kid.

This is what she wants more of.

This—

She wants this remembered, too. She wants to say, to the girl, *Remember? This was the story we lived.*

The thoughts of a dying woman are futile. They are selfish.

In the end they always leave, the family of five whooshed from the city, out to the suburbs by the creek, where the girl will take her book to read. In the end her son brings her a Whitman's Sampler box and together they pick through it, eat whichever chocolate pieces they please. While in the kitchen her husband stacks the dishes in the sink, the elastic bands around his biceps keeping the cuffs of his shirtsleeves dry and neat.

Have a Whitman's, she calls to her husband. But the water gushes from the kitchen tap, louder than the sounds across the alley, and now she is rocking in her cushioned chair, rocking back

And—

Lani

isn't right. Walking wrong on South Twenty-third. That isn't walking. She's dragging one hand against the faces of the brick houses, barely supporting herself in the gap places, the empty air where there are stoops, or a bike tossed up against a wall. Peggy catches a glimpse from her perch on the stoop reading the old news, then looks up for real and there is Lani, bent and wrong and blundering home, walking the one side of South Twenty-third and not the other, like she normally does. Lani walking like she doesn't know which side her life is on.

"Ma!" Peggy calls, through the door, because she already knows she can't do this alone, and Harry is working overtime, and Jennie's out with her two best girls, and the others are where they are, Pops upstairs having an after-dinner snooze.

Whatever has happened to Lani will need two, at least, to fix, and now Ma's coming and Peggy's running, shouting Lani's name out loud, as if the sound of her voice can keep Lani from falling down hard, as if Hannah, outside with a piece of chalk, has not stood and stared, then rushed inside, her hands over her eyes so that she cannot further see.

Then, more softly, Peggy calls. Closer, Peggy comes. She is almost there now, she has Lani.

"I've got you," Peggy says. "I've got you."

Catching Lani in her arms, Lani's limbs loose as a skein of yarn. Lani has walked this far, she can't keep walking, she's going to fall, slam to the walk, break farther and farther apart. Lani like this is Lani heavier than Lani is, now in Peggy's arms. Peggy, who stumbles back, but holds. Some more children coming out onto the street to take a look. An old man smoking a cigar, scowl on his face, he's not one to help. The pansies in the flower boxes folding their faces back. The knitting needles stopping.

"Peggy," Lani sobs.

Her lip busted or burst and her voice, too. Her nose leaking blood. One eye already so swollen shut Peggy doesn't know how Lani found her way to almost home. Must have felt her way here, brick by brick. All of Lani's extra weight on Peggy. All of the broken in the way she breathes, in the short inhaling sniffs of air and the erratic, ragged exhales. Peggy holds her steady, *now, now,* until Ma appears.

"Whatever?" Ma starts, and then she stops, only:

"One arm over my shoulder, Love. One arm over Peggy's. Can you do that for us? Can you, Lani?"

Lani says she can.

They straighten her out—Ma on one side, Peggy on the other. They lift and stutter-step Lani home, to their house. Lani's head dropped down and small beads of blood splatting the walk, or Lani's boot, or the apron Ma still has on, her after-dinner wear. Lani so close that Peggy can smell the sugar in her teeth, the coconut in her twisted hair, the violence that's been done. The rust smell of the drying blood.

"You'll be all right," Ma says, encouraging.

"Yes," Peggy says. "It's all right, Lani. Just another block and we'll be home."

"Mother can't— " Lani exhales. "Don't tell. Please."

She is out of tears. She is only gasp.

Peggy catches Ma's eye across Lani's drooped head. Catches her nod. Yes. Suddenly understands that Lani was heading toward Peggy all along, that the wrong side of the street was the right side of the street, given what's been done. What *has* been done, and who has done it to Lani?

"We'll get you all fixed up," Ma is saying, reaching across herself with her free hand to tuck Lani's dark hair behind her ear, to begin the slow repair.

They are half a block now. They are three houses away, now two. Three little girls walking behind them. A boy with a stick behind them. Now Hannah. Then, at the stoop, they all stop. Ma and Peggy lift Lani up the three steps of their stoop, the blood of her still splatting. They ease Lani into the closest chair, and Ma kneels down to remove Lani's boots. "Go run the bath," Ma says to Peggy, and Peggy races up the stairs, shoves the drying laundry aside, opens the tap for Lani.

"You let it go now," Peggy hears Ma downstairs. "You cry as much as you want. We'll get you all fixed up."

"Mother can't," Lani gasps. "Mother—"

"I'll take care of it, Lani. I will. But tonight we are taking care of you."

Fiction (Non-)

The house on South Twenty-third is still where it was, brick-red paint thick on the real brick. Charcoal-colored grit on the white window frames, the frames too big for the windows now, waterlogged and gurgled. Three stoop steps that look like minor coffins that have been zaggedly stacked.

Of the two grates bolted across the narrow basement windows, one is half-cocked, the other maimed by a kick of wild ivy. A black scrap of tar paper has fallen from the roof to the street, and so it stays.

In this story things happen when they must. Where.

When the girl who will grow up to be a writer calls her son and reads to him from the opening pages of this book she intends as her grandmother's book, the book her grandmother might have written, he will ask her what it is.

"You mean?"

"I mean it's almost all true and it's almost all fiction." He'll say. "But which one is it?"

"Yes," she'll say, "that's what it is."

When the girl who grows up will ask her brother if he knows anything at all about the shop at Fifty-second and Market Streets, he will say that he knows nothing except that he remembers.

"You remember what?"

"Being there."

"You? There?"

"I was young, very young. The memory is a four-second flash."

"Am I there?" The grown-up girl will ask. "Inside your memory?" Ask with fervor. Ask with the cinema reel of the history of yearning, "Among My Souvenirs" on the Victrola, playing. And the weather streaming. And the spin of the whisk of her wishing.

Go on. No stopping now. The war is on them.

The smell of the rust in her.

The claw-footed tub full of its slosh. Peggy and Ma, helping Lani sink down, the bloodstains in the water now, but floating.

"Nice and easy," Ma says. "Water's your friend."

"I'm American," Lani blubbers. "True as him."

"Yes," Ma says. "Yes, now, Lani. Bits of glass, here, Lani. Going to tweeze the glass parts out. You close your eyes. You squeeze the sponge. Nothing but a minute now."

And Lani does—closes her eyes, squeezes the sponge—because crying would make the hurt hurt more, and she won't hurt more, the slow dark bruise, now, of Lani's resolve. The black coarse curls, too, letting themselves down, all the way down, streamers of dark running her shoulders, and Ma sits on the edge of the porcelain tub and Peggy sits on the rough wooden lid of the toilet, stitching the strap back onto Lani's slip with a too-dark thread, a little tighter this time, so the strap won't slide down, enough of that, now, Lani, and Lani knows it.

"I told him I'm no girl like that," Lani begs, wincing now as Ma digs another shard out of the flesh of her arm.

"Broke a bottle on you, didn't he, Love," Ma says, and Lani nods.

"I fought him," she says, "with every noise I had."

"You did good, Lani," Ma says. "Real good," and Lani nods. But none of them knows how far up the bleeding goes, if the tub water, cool now, can stop it.

They hear Jennie coming up the stairs, then Harry, then another, another. Each time Pops appears at the top of the steps and warns them off the second floor. "We have a visitor," Pops says, and that's all he says, knowing it to be female business.

That night Lani, wearing Peggy's sleeping dress, sleeps on Peggy's part of the bed, with Peggy's sisters. Her damp hair creeps a stain across Peggy's part of the pillow. When she's settled in, closing both eyes now and not just the one with the bruising, Peggy slips outside in the dark, and across the street, to tell Lani's mother the truth—that Lani has come over for a visit, and she will be fine, she will be home tomorrow.

"Okay, now," Lani's mother says, all the narrow arrows in her upper lip pointing down and frightened. She doesn't ask a single question, doesn't invite Peggy in for more, and Peggy is glad for her bottled-up discretion, glad to play her part in not disclosing, keeping her promise to Lani. Lying like this is good Christian.

"Here," Ma says, when Peggy comes back, steps through the front door with the moon on her, the moon still coming in through the front window. Ma hands Peggy the top edge of the Irish blanket they keep as extra in Ma's trunk. Peggy takes her seat in the upholstered chair made big enough for two. Ma stands for a little while more, rubs at the small of her back, loosens her shoes. Then she takes her place beside Peggy and sighs, her apron crinkling up in her lap. The chill is the chill of evening April. Their bodies are close now, keeping each other warm, beneath the woolen blanket.

"She'll be all right?" Peggy asks, turning to see the silhouette of her mother's face, in the stolen moon of the night's darkness.

"Hmmm," Ma says, and Peggy knows. No more now, no more questions. Tomorrow's a church day and they'll go to pray: For the doughboys. For the family. For Lani.

Dear—

If he were not gone to Camp,

not regimenting.

If he were not where she does not know enough about it to imagine. Camp Meade. South. Gun polish. Boot muck. A big outdoor clock with the measure of the Liberty Loans drawn on it. Someone always shouting. Over hill over dale beyond the yonder.

If her letters were to reach him. If her letters now were private. How could her letters now be private? Tucked into his bag, tucked into his sheets, swipe his pillow, they will find them. Peggy cannot, most absolutely cannot tell him about Lani. Peggy wants him to come home so she can tell him about Lani. Wants him to come home so that he will be home, here, beside her. Away from the making way for war. Out of tomorrow's headlines.

She would say. She would talk. He would listen. Breathe through the split in his teeth. Bring her a fresh Sampler after a day full of worsteds and beneath the lid of the Whitman's box would be the Rudyard Kipling stories, Little Library treasure. In the early parts of the evenings, when there would be light enough, when Hannah and the girls three houses down would be jumping rope and the boys a little farther off knuckle-boning, Peggy would read the Kipling out loud to him, because she'd already read to him from the Emerson, and already read to him through the end of that portrait of that artist, which was a strange book indeed, but she cannot lose its pattern, its way of speaking, its way of pressing on the ways that she is thinking. She would read the Kipling to him by way of reading it to Lani, and Lani, across the street, in her second-floor bed, would listen. The window open. The curtain empty. The strap of the pale-blue slip tight now on Lani's shoulder. Peggy imagining what she couldn't see, which was Lani lying awake on her own pillow, counting how far and wide is the enemy, the Germans over there and the Germans over here, the more war there is, the more enemies, and you cannot be the enemy, you can't say what you want: No war.

If he would just come home, other boys come home. If she could just go to him, but Peggy is not a mother, wife, or sister.

May 16, 1918: The Sedition Act

Section III: Whoever, when the United States is at war, shall willfully make or convey false reports or false statements with intent to interfere with the operation or success of the military or naval forces of the United States, or to promote the success of its enemies, or shall willfully make or convey false reports, or false statements, ... or incite insubordination, disloyalty, mutiny, or refusal of duty, in the military or naval forces of the United States, or shall willfully obstruct ... the recruiting or enlistment service of the United States, or ... shall willfully utter, print, write, or publish any disloyal, profane, scurrilous, or abusive language about the form of government of the United States, or the Constitution of the United States, or the military or naval forces of the United States ... or shall willfully display the flag of any foreign enemy, or shall willfully ... urge, incite, or advocate any curtailment of production ... or advocate, teach, defend, or suggest the doing of any of the acts or things in this section enumerated and whoever shall by word or act support or favor the cause of any country with which the United States is at war or by word or act oppose the cause of the United States therein, shall be punished by a fine of not more than $10,000 or imprisonment for not more than 20 years, or both .....

Dear—

Peg?

She hears her husband's voice from across the years.

He's near now. She can smell him. She wonders what he'll eat tonight, if he's hungry.

He straightens the sheets. He delivers the wooden bed tray with the painted flowers and the peg legs. He puts upon it a turquoise glass, which he has filled with water. A quite tall turquoise glass. With ice. The ringing of the bells of ice.

Her husband is not a small man, but he moves like a foxtrotter. Feather step. Feather finish. Shoulders down to make momentum. He calls his stomach The Corporation. Where it leads, he follows. No creak in his knees, the *whish* of his polish, he always keeps his leathers polished. His hair has turned white as she's lain dying. He's never lost its perfect part, the shine of the Bryl in it.

He won't be getting old. He will be enduring, a Sicilian, a good dresser. He will always have been the top Prudential salesman. Even when there was nothing, before Franklin D. and the Deals he made, her husband would come home with something (she repeats herself, she wishes to re-member this, the heart of the man that she married)—a square of fabric, a brand-new needle, a head of garden lettuce, a borrowed book for her to read, instead of policy pay. When no one had policy pay, he'd still come home with something, *Take this,* his customers would say, and *Next time.*

Now is his *Next time.* When she is gone, and soon she will be, her hus-band will go dancing, polish the floor with the slick of his shoes, touch another woman with the need of his hands. But for now he brings her water in a turquoise glass, ice music, the peg-legged tray to set it on, above her lap, get ready. He calls her name before he knocks on the door, *her* door, he sleeps alone in the back bedroom. Knocks on the door and calls her—

Peg?

His name for her in her life of names. Margaret. Peggy. Peg.

Collecting her good marks at school as Margaret. Signing her name to marriage as Margaret. Casting her vote for Hope and for Franklin D. as Margaret. Putting her name onto the deed for the house where she lies in her bed as Margaret.

Peggy was for Ma and Pops and Harry and Jennie, for the boy with the split in his teeth. Peg for her husband. Mrs. at church and the corner stores, at the shop that she provisioned with her son, that pearl of a gift shop, those running ribbons, Easter baskets.

Mom for her son, for her daughter.

Aunt for the one who will write a few spare lines onto two pages and slip the pages in a box where they will go for nearly thirty years silent and hibernating. Pages that will, in the end, be found—the exposé of three precipitating lines: *She worked at Fleisher's at 26ᵗʰ and Reed Sts. in Philadelphia. I think it was a textile or clothing company.*

Grandmom for the one who is remembering the story she imagines her remembering—feathers in her pocket, Little Libraries, the hands that run the Triumph.

Peg?

If she answers she is still on the side of the living.

Girls Wanted,

the papers say.

Silk winders at Sauquoit's. Burlers in the weaving shed at Hardwick and Magee's. Stenographers at the Sugar House and welders at Hog Island and gear grinders at Midvale Steel and incendiary-bullet loaders at the Frankford Arsenal and compositors at Curtis Publishing and ticket takers at Lubin's Palace down at Eleventh and Market.

Loretta Walsh has enlisted in the U.S. Navy and hundreds more girls are taking up arms, and there's a Women's Land Army hoeing liberty gardens into vacant lots to help feed the people working at home to feed the doughboys, and now here Peggy is, standing beneath the Grecian frieze at Twenty-sixth and Reed, wearing Jennie's best dress loose at the shoulders and short by the knees and Harry's extra bowler low on her brow, neither of them missing either on this cool, bright day in May, nobody guessing where she is. Had she told them, they'd have stopped her. She was their book girl, their school star, their pride amongst the family.

"Going somewhere," Ma always said, thinking maybe one day Peggy'd be a teacher. *Their* Peggy. Think of it.

"Love you," she'd called out to Ma when she left, plucking a few dying pansy faces from the window box before she made her way. Calling out *Morning* to Lani, whose bedroom window was opened just a crack to let the new air of the day in. Peggy had waited. No *Morning* back. No sign of Lani for all these weeks now. She was going to have to talk to Lani. Tomorrow she would. After this thing she would do for herself.

Her boots polished. Her nails squared. Her schoolbag empty but looped across her chest. For the show of it. For nobody guessing.

She stands to the side, lets the workers rush in. She rehearses her interview plan. She'll tell them what she knows about yarn, to begin. The short, wild fibers of the regular wool, she'll say. The long parallel combing of the worsted. She'll sit with a proper straight back, both feet on the floor, and repeat what she'd read in the catalogue the boy had carried with him and shared with her on her stoop, at the Automat, in Wharton Square. How the wool moves from the sheep to the sorter to the duster to the scourer to the dryer to the dyers to the carders and the combers. How after that it makes its way—chutes, he'd read out loud, conveyor belts—to the self-acting mule, such a funny name, which the boy could not get over. The five-foot gallop of the mechanical thing. Back and forth across the factory floor it went, spindling the roving, filling the bobbins, waiting for the doffers, and that would be her.

GIRLS WANTED FOR DOFFING

All her skills in her mind, from a book. Everything she knows a theory, but that is more knowing than most, maybe, and it has to be enough to get the job, which pays $6.50 a week, or so she's read in the classifieds that come after the headlines. She had torn that part of the paper free and stuffed it in her pocket, because it could have been any neighbor on her street who'd gotten the thump of news first on their stoop, opened to that spread, and torn. Nobody, not even Pops, would suspect her.

Every time the door opens she hears the thrum of things inside. When it closes she hears the traffic on the street. It's getting to be ridiculous.

Do it or don't.

In or out.

She opens the door. She's in.

The smell of it first—lanolin and grease, grass and machines. The sound second, like the trains overhead at the Reading Market, where the boy's father has less and less to sell and less and less to say when she does her Saturday shopping. She sees the boy in her mind, remembers the first time she saw him, an apron tied at his waist and his hands beautiful with rhubarb, and how he felt her staring and looked up, and didn't mind.

The luck in it.

The employment office is on the sixth floor and up by way of elevator. Peggy follows the dozens, pretends she belongs, tries not to look like it's her first time, but it is her first time, in an elevator. She waits for the others to climb into the cab. Someone does the buttons like it's nothing. She is asked, polite, "Sixth floor?" And she nods. Better get her voice back, better get the jump out of her chest.

"Sixth floor. Please." There. She's said it.

Straightens Jennie's dress with her hands. Removes Harry's hat, which she brought for good fortune, but what should she do with it now?

Stuff it in her schoolbag. Worry the crush of it later. Make it up to Harry when she gets the job and has money of her own to pay.

There's a line but not a long one—men older than Pops, girls younger than her, a portly woman who might be thirty. Peggy takes her place but stands apart. She takes a longer breath to calm herself and thinks how it is to be standing inside the vastness of the kingdom of textiles, the complex she and the boy had watched from the street, going up higher and higher. In the Workshop of the World that is her city this must be the finest workshop, with gleam in the windows and height in the ceilings and art hanging on the walls in simple maple frames.

Like a museum, she thinks.

Peggy steps a little closer to the art to understand. She reads the little placards. The names of the artists are the names of those who belong to Mr. Samuel Fleisher's Graphic Sketch Club down on Catharine Street. Everybody knows about the Sketch Club—open all day and also at night, and open for free to the factory workers and their children wanting to paint, design, or dance. Samuel Fleisher, son of the original Simon B. Fleisher and now in charge, or partly in charge, of this entire place.

It's because of him, she's read, that there's a library at Fleisher's. And musical concerts on Wednesday evenings. And a piano in the lounge. And a dining room big enough to seat one thousand, which is just like Horn & Hardart, where the rich who are the managers sit with the poor who do the work.

Peggy wants this job at Fleisher's.

She sees a future in it.

She's next. She's now. She's shaking Mrs. Velma Martine's hand, and noticing her knitted dress—Fleisher yarn and a Fleisher pattern. She's noticing how her hair's cut short and how the ribbon tied around her neck has nothing dangling from it. No cameo. No cut glass.

Peggy's spine never touches the spine of the chair. Her shoulders never slump. She answers the questions she's asked, polite and firm, and then she delivers on her plan, talking everything she knows about wool.

Then some.

When she takes a breath she notices Mrs. Martine's painted lips have relaxed into a smile. She hears the carding and the combing and the mules beneath her feet. She hears the rush of purpose through the chutes, the persistence of the new conveyor belts. She hears more than she can remember now, and then she stands and makes her way past the others who are waiting, and when she leaves she operates the elevator on her own.

Peggy is a brand-new Fleisher's doffer. She'll be starting in two weeks. She'll train under the direction of Miss Anne Theiler. She will report at eight.

She makes herself scarce for the rest of the day—touring the city like a stranger, having a solo coffee at Horn & Hardart, only a coffee, though soon she'll be able to afford more, soon she'll take Ma out for something

Ma didn't bake, see how that is, see how important it is to do for others when you have the money to do, when you're working on behalf of the war so you can bring the boy home, when you're stepping up: A citizen.

The next day,

Peggy makes her case. Lays it all out in after-class quiet with Mr. Walrath, Miss Bergmann, Mr. Stohr, Mrs. Rains, the other teachers whose names she can't remember, those who call her Margaret. A bargain is struck. They will tell Peggy what's ahead in school and Peggy will do the work, all of it, in two weeks' time, her quite best work. She will finish the year on her own terms, learn what is given, lose nothing according to her star-student standing, save this as good news for her mother.

Not leaving school, just going faster.

Not quitting learning, but beginning.

Every day after this one Peggy stays late to read the books, answer the questions, draw the math onto the board, take the corrections. Extra time and extra work. June lessons stuffed into May. Sometimes writing one essay on the back of another essay, and taking her words, teacher to teacher, to collect her approvals, and only now, remembering back, does it occur to her how openhanded her teachers had been and what a privilege it had been to be privileged. Doing it for her, is what they did, bending the rules and working the administration, respect to the girl who had respected them and carried home their teachings. Raised her hand. Answered questions.

Making new rules for her when all else was broken.

GIRLS FOR DOFFING

There is no going back. There is no reversing her decision. On Monday Peggy will start her job at Fleisher's, take an apron, report to Mrs. Vasey, who will send her to Miss Theiler, and then Peggy will stand on her feet for most of the day. It's good that her high-tops are eased with walking. Though by now her secret, this job at Fleisher's, is so swollen big that at night, at whatever dinner they are allowed on whatever Less day it is, she lets everyone else do the talking. Harry about his machines, and

Pops about the boots, and Jennie about the boy she is not so secretly seeing. Ma worrying.

But the not saying is lying, and lying isn't Peggy's number one skill. A long lie is a long rope, and around Peggy's thoughts it tightens.

It's to Pops that she decides to do the telling.

She remembers walking beside her father, in the sun. It's the Saturday before the Monday when she'll begin her doffing. Pops is working his double shift. The back of his shirt is wet with sweat. His hand is on the handkerchief inside his pocket. Down the stoop they have gone, and down the street, on the way to the Arsenal, Peggy carrying Pops's pail.

The work of the war beneath his nails and in the thin gray envelopes of skin beneath his eyes. She mentions the end of pansy season and the newest song. She remembers both of them talking the headlines, eyes straight ahead, just her and Pops, but every block they walk is a block less she has for talking, and Peggy is running out of time. She has to say what she is here to say, her rationales and reasons.

She'll say:

She's left the school year early because it's time to get the doughboys home, because if she can do this part, then she will do it.

She'll say:

The teachers have agreed. Mrs. Rains, especially, who stayed on in the afternoon to quiz Peggy on the facts of the American Revolution—the British Army, the Loyalists, the Hessians—then stopped the quizzing halfway through to talk the present battles.

She'll say:

Mrs. Rains is young and her husband is enlisted, training in the same camp as Peggy's boy. In the classroom empty but for the two of them,

Peggy talked to Mrs. Rains, who sat at her desk in front of the scratch of the chalkboard while Peggy sat at the soft wood of a first-row table, where one of the girls had dug out a heart with her fingernail. Peggy tracing that heart as Mrs. Rains, her chin cradled in one hand, looked away, toward the window, and talked.

She'll tell

that story to Pops to make a good of the news she knows in her heart he will not see the good in.

"Doing my part," Peggy repeats herself, now, in memory, to her Pops. But Pops keeps on walking, looking straight ahead, the early sun rising behind them. His shadow at his feet. Her shadow at hers. She is taller, she suddenly realizes, than he is. The windows are being pulled up in the houses as they pass. The sound of tea kettles is coming through, tired arguments, a little girl crying, a piano playing itself.

"It's what I want," Peggy says. She squeezes a fist in her sweater pocket to bulk her confidence, swings his lunch pail with her other hand. "I thought a lot about it."

"How long?" is what he asks.

"Pops?"

How long has she been keeping the secret from them, he means.

"Just a few weeks, Pops."

He shakes his head. He lifts the white square of his handkerchief to the bottom of one ear to catch the pool of sweat that's started dripping. It's not that hot, but Pops is like this—a small man overheating.

The more Peggy talks the less he does. The more she talks the more she wishes there was less that she was saying. She got extra credit for her special report on James Joyce's rhythms, she says. She got more history with Mrs. Rains alone than had she been sitting with the others in the class.

"Like private tutoring, Pops. That's what it was."

Onto Washington Avenue now, heading west. Down the widest width of street. The pushcart vendors, the kids in their bare feet, and down the curb into the street. Back up the next curb, out of the street. Around a couple of hounds and their men. A woman smoking cigarettes slouches against a wall, like it's the start of the night for her.

"Your Ma would have wanted—" Pops starts. "School being your future—" he starts again.

"Everybody doing their part, Pops," Peggy says. "And I still have my future."

"You, Pops," Peggy says. "You're doing more than your part."

"That's my business," Pops says. "As your father."

The trolley goes past on its thin rails, its sign advertising Proverbs XII:19. A boy who's Peggy's age runs, desperate for a seat, but the trolley goes on, a racket on rails, and they're almost there, Peggy and Pops at the Arsenal, where Washington Avenue disappears into the swerve of Gray's Ferry. Not enough windows in the brick where Pops works. Not enough light for his eyes. All night long Pops rubs his eyes, like rubbing will help improve the speed with which he sees the soles he'll bang into place the next day. The money she'll make could help Pops, too, put less strain on him, cut his overtiming.

She'll make the larger difference working, Peggy tries to say, new words for the same argument. She'll change the headlines they both read a few days late. She'll be on the front lines in the Workshop of the World, help bring the doughboys home. She'll stop the Germans over there from hurting the Germans over here. *Lani,* she wants to say. Look what they've done to Lani.

She'd wanted a job, she remembers now, and she got a job, at Fleisher's. Where not just Samuel is doing good for the world, but his brother, too. A yarn factory run by philanthropists. They've got a baseball team. A piano. A library. Fleisher's is the future. Peggy's casting her lot with it.

"Prettiest new building in the city, Pops," Peggy says, turning her head to look at him now, wondering how long it's been since she's stood taller than him. If he's that old now. If he is shrinking. If it is hotter than she thinks it is. Why else, this overheating?

They are almost there, at the Arsenal. Up a curb, down one, Pops's lunch pail in Peggy's hand. The two of them are coming to the place where this walking ends, turning to one another. A ray of sun catches a broad spot in the left lens of his spectacles.

"I can't argue with it," he finally says. "Your ma will wish you told her sooner."

"I know, Pops."

"She'll wish you'd trusted her with your decision. Told her before you conspired with the teachers. Everybody but us you told. That isn't like the Finleys."

"It wasn't conspiring."

"You kept it a secret."

Even then, she realizes now, feeling light in her bed, light, as if she's elevating, as if she's transcending what she remembers now, so radically, no stopping the memories flowing. Even then she kept her secrets.

Pops reaches his hand toward hers. Takes his pail. Last night's stew and a wedge of pie, which he'll eat cold, sometime past noon, staying to himself, as he does, a lonesome job in a crowd of men, the hammering of boots. Peggy dips her knees to kiss his cheek.

"You'll help me tell Ma, then," she says, putting no question mark at the end of her sentence and not seeing his eyes for the sun.

"You'll do all the talking," he says.

"I'm sorry, Pops," she says.

"You make us proud at Fleisher's."

There's the sound of the factory in her ear. The sound of the knitting needles clacking as she heads east toward the day's chores—the laundry, then the market, the parsley, parsnips, radishes, rhubarb. She'll see the boy's father and he'll have hardly any news and she'll stand there, taking longer than she needs to choose what he'll send back home with her.

Peg?

her husband calls.

I am, she says, *here.*

But don't disturb her,

because now that she is remembering she is remembering the look on Ma's face that particular evening long ago, feels like right now, what is the difference? She is remembering Pops, his shirt full of the smell of leather and tools. She is remembering what Harry said, sitting there at the kitchen table, a chill in the air for it was late at night and Jennie was already in bed upstairs, or gossiping, among the others. Harry's cigarette was smoking above them. His hand was on his heart.

"Peggy's still the smart one, Ma," Harry said. "Peggy's still going somewhere."

Her mother pushed back her chair, stood and left the room, took nothing with her. She opened the door and went out onto the stoop where there was already a blue pour of moon. When Peggy opened the door to sit beside her, Ma shook her head and raised one hand.

"Leave me, Peggy," she said.

Words you never do forget, when your mother says them.

"Lani?"

Peggy calls out into Sunday evening's gloaming, another Little Leather in her lap. "You listening?"

It's the day after the night when Ma was told. At church Ma sat stiff and quiet beside her, not singing the hymns, not saying the Lord Is My Shepherd. Jennie and the others had stayed in bed and Harry was at Baldwin's and Pa was resting. On the way back home, Ma put her hand on Peggy's shoulder.

"You be careful. That's what I ask. And do less secret keeping."

"Lani?" Peggy calls again. Waits. Watches the kids down the street playing their game of marbles. Hannah in charge of all marble things. And Hannah also watching.

Now Lani's hand appears in the second-floor window, fingers closed into a fist, like a periscope coming up from the sea. Peggy sees it, from the corner of her eye.

"Come outside," Peggy raises her chin so Lani can hear her better. "Hurts my voice, reading so loud."

"Didn't ask you to read now, did I?"

The low muffle of Lani's voice comes from the pillow beneath the window.

Just like that, no more beat to it, Peggy thrusts herself up off the stoop and lowers the blades of her shoulders. Shoves Rudyard Kipling into her sweater pocket, fixes the feathers beside him. Marches across the walk, across the street, and across the opposite walk. Marches those twelve long steps to Lani's front door, her skirt full of whoosh. Doesn't stop for knocking, bangs straight through, says hello to the widowed Mrs. who is a slump of half-sleep on the first-floor armchair, her head fallen back on a knitted doily, her mouth wide open.

Peggy climbs the long stairs to the second floor, marches the short steps toward Lani's room and turns the knob of the door. Pushes in. Catches Lani fighting to pull the sheets over her body, as if Peggy hadn't sat just two months ago on her own toilet seat while Ma bathed Lani naked, draining the rust from the water, saying *there, there, there.*

"You've got to get back to the living," Peggy says. "Back to Whitman's. Coconuts need you." Insistent, Peggy knows for certain what her friend must do to get herself better, and then, in the stroke of an instant, she sees what Lani has been reading—the Mary Mills West book, published by the Children's Bureau, which explains all the rules of baby caring. Lani shoves the book out of sight, under the sheets, so Peggy can't see what she's already seen. All the charged-up Irish in her breaks inside one instant.

"Aw, Lani," Peggy says. "Lani."

"I can't," Lani says.

"What is it, Hon?" Peggy says, as if she needs to ask the question.

"Looks like what it is," Lani says, sobbing. "A baby coming."

"You sure?"

Lani says she's sure. Shakes her head back and forth and nods at the same confusing time.

Peggy reaches for Lani's hand beneath the sheets, reads her face for the shadow of the bruise, sees the loose threads at the base of Lani's strap, the strap will come off if Peggy doesn't try, again, to fix it. "Lani, Honey," Peggy says, now taking her friend into her arms.

"Couldn't hurt me enough so he left me like this," Lani says. "Everything," she says. "Everything is ruined." She sobs so hard Peggy's arms cannot contain her. The bed is too weak. The bed cannot contain her.

"Honey," Peggy says again, her mind working the calculations. A baby coming in September, in October? A baby with no pa and no right-minded grandmother to help lift the baby up, to coo her, the baby already being a girl in Peggy's mind, a baby with a mother who will have no job at Whitman's to feed her, a mother who hasn't smelled like sugar since she stumbled up Peggy's side of the street and Peggy helped to bathe her.

The bubble of snot in Lani's nose breaks when she breathes in again. "Ma doesn't know," she tells Peggy. "And I won't tell her."

"Course not," Peggy says. "Shhhh."

But she knows it won't be long before Lani won't have to be saying any words; her body will be doing all the speaking for her. Her body in the house will be the proof of what has happened. Her body on the street will be a soiled dove or a scarlet lady, a calico queen or a sporting girl, and she'll still be German and it will still be a crime to teach the language of where she came from in school, still a fact that German measles are now Liberty measles and sauerkraut is now Liberty cabbage and the statues of Goethe and Bismarck have been patriot-ruined with thick drownings of yellow paint, and what kind of good man will have her?

"You have money?" Lani asks Peggy now, "to spare?"

"What for, Lani?" Peggy releases her hold somewhat.

Lani shrugs.

"What for, Lani?" Peggy asks again.

"Pennyroyal?" Lani says it, quiet as a whisper, as if the police could hear. "Turpentine?"

"Shhh," Peggy says. "Don't say that. Be the death of you."

"*This* is the death of me."

Lani breaks herself free of Peggy's hold, lets the book of Mary Mills West drop to the floor. She sits straighter in the bed, bangs the tears from her face with her fists, shows off her resolve. "I'll do it, Peggy," she says. "One way or the other. I swear."

"It's a baby," Peggy says. "It's you."

"It's what he did," Lani says. "Baby has nothing to do with me."

And Peggy knows she's right, and she knows how women die—drinking the pennyroyal and the turpentine. "You'll get through," Peggy says, though she doesn't know how.

"He called me Kaiser," Lani says. "He called me Kaiser all the way in."

"Who?" Peggy asks, her voice small. "Who did this to you, Lani?"

"Two of them," Lani says.

Peggy shudders. "Two, Lani?"

"Waiting for me in the alley not far from Whitman's. I couldn't run fast enough to beat them."

Lani stops, collects herself, says what it was like and it's the first time she ever said it. It's the first time, Peggy suddenly knows for sure, that she's ever said it: "They yanked me into the back of a car. The second one held me down, kept saying Kill the Kaiser. I screamed. I screamed bloody everything. Somebody must have heard me. Nobody would help me."

"No," Peggy says. "Oh, Lani."

"It's not my baby," Lani says. "You have to help me."

Peggy never heard a moan like that. It's how her cancer sounds, when Peg remembers.

Milk and eggs,

she hears her husband call now. *And I'll buy the paper.*

The door opens and shuts behind him.

She closes her eyes, chases sleep, opens her eyes again.

The silver mirror strikes the sun, or the sun strikes the silver mirror, and she hears the clink, and she is all alone, again.

I can't do this, she thinks. I can't keep on with the remembering. I can't.

But if she does not remember, what is she? Who? If she does not remember, what are these hours now, her final hours? Who? She closes her eyes, and her mind gentles. She keeps her eyes closed and time rearranges itself, just like that, for her sake. Memory returns her to the kinder year, to 1917, when, all of a sudden, easy as that, it is summer, and the best day of her life.

Willow Grove Park and

Harry and Ma and the boy.

Willow Grove Park and—

there it is:

the four of them together, catching the open-air summer trolley at Chestnut and Sixteenth. Harry doing most of the talking. Ma laughing like someone set her free—a bird without a cage. The boy touching the back of Peggy's hand with the back of his hand when no one else was looking and the way she could hardly stand it, the way she yearns to feel it now, the ghost of a sensation.

The crowd with them.

The trolley moving.

They rode the thirteen miles into everything becoming green. And the air clean. And the houses beyond the trolley line like palaces of horticulture, blooming and refined. And did you ever see such a thing, and she can see it now, she can almost feel it.

It was the boy's birthday. The party had been Harry's idea and the money was money Harry'd stashed in a sock. The shoebox lunches were Ma's making—lettuce and tomato sandwiches on hard heels of bread, and a pie made out of strawberries, and some cheese, because the boy liked cheese. The boy did all the carrying—had brought a wooden crate from the market stand to put the soft-boxed lunches in. Looked like an accordion grinder when he walked, the box going everywhere before him.

It'd been the president of the Union Traction Company who'd bought the land out there by the mineral springs. It'd been Peter Widener and William Elkins who'd done the original distributing of the Nickel Scenic, the Shoot the Chutes, and the Captive Flying Machine; the airy pavilions and the picnic groves; the lanes of flower gardens; the massive man-made lake with the tower of a fountain that gushed water and color at the same time; the ladies' comforts.

Though the first thing they'd see when the trolley stopped was The Alps, that domination of a mountainscape built of wood and painted burlap. A coaster train, it was said, which rode the mountain tracks to the panoramic view then plunged inside the carved-out tunnels, which were dark except for the pretty grottoes and the scenery somebody had imagined.

You could ride the canals of Venice at the Park. You could watch the mechanical coal miners work from your seat in a coal miners' coaster. You could take a tour of the world in railway cars that agitated back and forth while movies reeled on a screen before you. Real movies, of the real world, and you would be there, watching. She'd read about it, they all had, and now their trolley had stopped and they were there at the Park, and Ma had to stop and step away from the crowd and catch her breath from the thrill.

"Did you ever?"

No.

As if it couldn't have been, but maybe it was; it was.

She hears the sound of her own lungs, breathing. Still, the air in them.

The boy is just in front of where Ma and Peggy are standing. The crate is in his hands. He is a head shorter than Harry, straight beside him as if they are brothers. The crowds crush past, hands and hats shading the eyes of disbelievers. It is like standing in a windstorm and not knowing where the sounds come from—the rife rumble of the coasters on the tracks, the tin music of the carousel, the unloosened cries of children— and John Philip Sousa and his band are in the Park. At the matinee they will start playing.

The boy turns and catches Peggy's eye. Harry looks back over his shoulder, grinning. Ma unties the ribbon at her neck, for it is warm, the sun still rising.

They will eat their lunch in the picnic grove.

They will row rented boats to the fountain.

They will take a ride on a painted horse, the boy leaving Harry with the empty crate, so that he can hold her from behind, on the horse they'll share, which is blue with a yellow mane. His arms warm through his shirt sleeves. His chest damp. That heat in her, rising.

The sound of her heart in the pulse in her ear, her noisy one companion.

Around and around on the painted horse. She will die before her granddaughter knows her story.

Though one day

(years on)

a box will be brought to the granddaughter containing remnants of her grandmother's past. The box will be thirty years late in arriving. The box will be—or is it *contain?*—genealogy and two typed pages titled "Among My Souvenirs." Words written by the grandmother's niece. Actual words. Actual history.

These are just a few "snippets" from a time before you knew her, the pages say.

Fleisher's, it says.

A wind-up Victrola.

1126 South Twenty-third.

Very pretty.

Accumulated Wisdom

The book's dark-green linen cover is threadbare and cracking. The pages inside are nearly translucent from your reading. Loose in the binding. The title is long: *The Pennsylvania Museum and School of Industry, Circular of the Philadelphia Textile School, Broad and Pine Streets.* "Read to us," some of the doughboys say at night, when they can't sleep for the ache in their bones, when only the sound of your voice going over the words in your yarn book can ease their mind toward nothing.

Proper nouns like a pendulum swinging:

All of this machinery was made especially for the school by the following well-known makers, and is up to date in every respect. It consists of revolving flat card, railway head and drawing frames from the Saco & Pettee Machine Works, Newton Upper Falls, Mass.; slubbing and roving frames from the Woonsocket Machine and Press Company, Woonsocket, R.I.

The whole bunch of the boys quieting down, as you say the words out loud. All those pleasing proper nouns:

warp and filling spinning frames from the Fales & Jenks Machine Co., Providence, R.I., and Whitin Machine Works, Whitinsville, Mass.; self-acting mule Platt Bro. Make, Oldham, Eng.; spooling, twisting, reeling and band making machinery, from the Easton & Burnham Machine Co. and Fales & Jenks Machine Co., Providence, R.I., and the Draper Company, Hopedale, Mass. The department is fully equipped with humidifiers from the American Moistening Company, Boston, Mass.

The other boys of the 314th Infantry Regiment, 79th Division are mostly from Pennsylvania anthracite, but some of them, like you, are born and bred Philadelphians. "Don't stop reading," they say, and even though you're tired now, you do read on, for your sake, for theirs.

Variations of cotton, you say.

Preparatory processes—bale breakers—mixing lattices—openers—intermediate and finisher pickers

Carding—construction and working of revolving flat cards, the necessary settings and adjustments

Card Clothing—Principles of grinding and practical accomplishments

One of the doughboys snorts. One of them is snoring.

Combing

Railway head—

Drawing—functions of the drawing frame

Fly frames—slubbers, intermediates, five roving frames, theory of winding

Spinning—the mule and ring frame, spindles, travelers, rings, building motions, calculations for draft and twist and production

If you can love a thing for the words of the thing, this is also why you love this thing. Or this, at least, is how I write it. Perpetually aware of the song in you, the music that you carry.

You've built your own log cabin nearby your regimental headquarters with these boys, no, who am I kidding—men. Your own officers' club and day room raised up and fortified from the parts of these trees that were still on all these acres growing. Horseshoe spikes as nails. Feed burlap as curtains. The thin rickety curve of wagon wheels as your fancy overhead light fixtures. You built it like you were overcome with frenzy, and then there it was, your own club, with a single shelf containing the collected decoratives and library.

You've gone into Odenton on the backs of mud-sucking trailers beside your fellow infantry, taking your hot meal and extra servings from the ladies of the Salvation Army. You've marked the one-year anniversary of America going into war on April 6 with a grand review in front of President Woodrow Wilson himself, a day remembered by historians as a most "remarkable showing." You've hitched a ride the whole ten miles to Laurel Park to watch the racing, got bored by the racing, and on a hot day of irritating training you and two more of you hoisted one of your own to Base Hospital No. 42 after the thick plug of a log in an obstacle course smacked him in the shin and snapped his ankle; you were paces ahead, and yet you heard it.

The flies have been thick from the manure that stinks to the almighty from the horses over at Remount Station 304, so you have hung more fly paper to the hoots and hollers of the boys with half their names, who start to call you their Interior Decorator, and then, one morning, while it is still dark and the day hasn't started and you haven't put yourself to sleep, you get up and march the distance to the horses, who, like you, have had no say in their drafting.

The smallest horses for the cavalry.

The medium horses for the light artillery.

The biggest horses for the siege batteries.

Most of the horses wearing bridles instead of halters and thin, because there never is enough straw or hay to feed them, and you don't think of it, you can't think of it, what it will be like when war is war, and not this training.

The freeloading flies. The goddam shit lovers.

You sit on your haunches for machine-gun training. You wait in long lines at the postal wearing the cape that doesn't fit you, gnawing on the last of the bread from Schmidt's Crusty delivery. You tuck your chin when the Hello Girls pass by, speaking their French and their English, but you don't squeeze out a tease with them like the others do, because there's a girl at home and she's waiting. Her picture's where your book is, between its pages. The one taken in the booth last summer on the day Harry took his savings out so that he could take the four of you to Willow Grove on a Sousa Day, when there'd be fireworks after the concert.

It wasn't even your birthday, that's the truth. It was Harry who had decided to make that day your day, or me, deciding for him. Harry who'd gone ahead and planned the adventure, out, away, from the city. And then he'd held that crate you'd been lugging all around so that you and the girl could get the picture treatment. Her hair is a little wild from the air it caught while you were rushing down the hills of the scenic railway. Her eyes are soft, like they were on the boat, when you paddled all the way out toward the fountain. There's the stain of some jam on her white collar in the picture and a coil of yarn knotted hard and fast and faithful around the pale flesh of her right wrist.

It was you who gave her that slip of ruby roving. You who tied it on her. She's still wearing that yarn, and it won't be coming off until you come home, which is the promise you made her.

When the trains

hiss-squawk above the Twelfth Street Market, and the cries of the brats are suffocated and the boasts of the farmers are trundled and you can't hear the coins that drop from your hands to the floor and so you lose them, and it's not this. When you rise and sink with the Scenic and dive and plunge with the Chutes and pierce the tunnels that have been carved out of the wood and burlap of the magic mountain, the tumult is froth and suds and irritated pleasure, but it is never this. The conveyor belts and troughs, the metal teeth and drums, the stampede of the self-acting mules, the persistence of the roving, the spinning of the spindles, the fallers rising, the fallers falling, the machinery that bolts to a start and slams to a stop and does the dragging, drawing.

There are 206 bones in her body—flat bones, irregular bones, short bones, long bones, sesamoid bones—and then there are her teeth. Standing here, in the Balling Department, every single hard part of Peggy is discomposed and rattled.

The air is thick with the spun-off flicks of wool that float and do not fall. The floor is littered with scatterings too heavy for the air to hold, though already, twice, the sweeper has come through, a tidying. A girl with red hair tucked into a blue bandana broadcasting fat white stars pushes the wheeled wooden carts where the empty bobbins go down between the long rows of the machines, toward Peggy. A boy wearing overalls three inches short passes by. The sound of the cart wheels coming in and out like an electrical storm that won't choose its own direction.

"You'll get used to it," Miss Theiler, queen of the doffers, says, when Peggy cups one ear to hear what she is saying, then, remembering manners, yanks her hand away.

Peggy stands up straight like Ma had told her, this morning, on the stoop, when she'd come outside to give Peggy a kiss goodbye, the hurt in Ma straining her jawline. "No more apologies," Ma'd said, as if any of the ones Peggy'd already offered had done any good, as if she could take it back, how she'd made her plan a secret. She thinks of Lani, pushing her window up at the same time as Ma's goodbye and waving her hand like a flag and how Peggy, hugging Ma and saying it again—"I'm sorry"—glimpsed the across-the-street sill with half an eye, thought at first that a dove had landed.

Then knew the flutter for what it was, and waved.

Ma hugged her again, then released her. She took the stoop down and headed south, looking back across her shoulder every couple of steps until she couldn't see Ma anymore and she couldn't see Lani's hands, and she was on her way to Fleisher's.

Safety is the first rule, Miss Theiler says. Appreciate the machines. Honor their power. Know them for their instincts, their unpersuadable mechanical minds. The electric belt for its lust. The metal teeth for their persistent hunger. The rapid whip of the spindles for their insatiability. You are to stand close enough to the moving carriage, but let the fallers do their business. You are to be alert to the stampede of the mules, their restless back and forth on their metal, tethered wheels, their five-foot trundling distance. One way, then the other, back then forth until the yarn is caught up on its bobbins. You are to be aware that yarn itself might seem a delicate thing—just twist and spin, slivers and threads, the fluff of sheep made useful—but the making of yarn is metal and grease and the people of Fleisher's who help the machines do their things.

"Midwifing," Miss Theiler says, and Peggy thinks of Lani.

"If you're a daydreamer, don't do your dreaming on your feet," Miss Theiler says. "Daydreaming is the number one enemy of safety. You a daydreamer?"

"No," Peggy says at once, with liar's speed.

"You'll have your breaks and you'll have your lunch. You do your dreaming then."

So, Peggy thinks. Miss Theiler sees.

Miss Theiler isn't tall, but she is blunt. She wears the metal frames of her half-spectacles high on the bridge of her nose, wears her hair in a quick, tight knot low on her neck. Her chin is solid. Her chest is wide. Her apron is officiously secured. Her skirt is from another fashion season, or, Peggy thinks, from no season at all, but it's Miss Theiler's hands that mark her. Their sudden surprising gentleness as they put on the show of what a good doffer does, which is to say remove the bobbins after they've been spun to their mechanical capacity and replace them with empty ones, which will be easy enough once, Miss Theiler says, Peggy gets the rhythm of it.

"Look," Miss Theiler says, "how it is." The mule carriage coming toward them now with the bobbins spinning quick. Now the carriage wheeling away. With every up and back the lines and lines of what is becoming yarn travel the distance from the drawing rolls to the spindles, and, around the bobbins, spins. The machine stops when the bobbins are full. The bobbins are released when the wound yarn is not too tight and not too loose, just perfect. Moving up and down the row, Miss Theiler fills the wooden carts with finished bobbins. The kid is back—agile, spry. Wheels the goods away. Now the girl comes by with a cart full of empties. Now the bobbins are replaced.

"See how it is?" Miss Theiler asks. "Try it for yourself."

So Peggy does. Her heart going double time, her bones thick with the sounds of machines, her fingers jerky with their wanting to do well, to hold up their part of the bargain. The promise she'd made to the boy.

The boy.

She feels his twist of yarn around her wrist. Touches the knot. Watches Miss Theiler step aside to fix another doffer's way of standing, reaching. Watches the mules going back and forth, the flecks flying, and thinks of that day in the park, when the boy stopped the walk they were on to take her hand with one of his, then dig into his pocket with his other. "Ten-ply," he'd said. "Rare as a ruby." It was that color, too, a bluster of red with a raspberry sheen to it. She lifted her palm up flat toward the sky. He tied it on, a good strong knot, the tips of his fingers brushing the quick blue jump of her pulse. She sparked.

"Close your eyes," she remembers him saying. "Don't move." And so she stood there in the park while the pigeons cooed and the sun got buried behind some clouds and the yarn on her wrist took the curve of her wrist; she felt the shift of weather. She stood and heard a kid run past, chasing a kite, it seemed, though she didn't open her eyes to find out, didn't open her eyes to see the boy digging into a bag he'd been carrying all along. She knew at once what it was when he placed his second find across her palm: the cool sculpted weight of his grandfather's bugle.

"Practice," he said. "When I'm gone."

Opened her eyes.

"But."

"When I come home," he said, "I'll expect a full-grown song."

"Now," Miss Theiler is back from where she'd gone and saying something Peggy didn't hear the start of. *You a daydreamer?* "If you spy some fray while the mule is moving," Peggy is sure she's saying now, "you'll need to give the roving a fresh twisting."

Miss Theiler makes a motion with her hand, to demonstrate in theory. She waits for a split to show and Peggy waits beside her, hiding her hand in the pocket of her Fleisher's apron and practicing the gesture. Doesn't take long before Miss Theiler spies some fray. Points, and Peggy nods. Yes, Peggy says. She sees. Now Miss Theiler walks forward with the mule as the mule retreats, Miss Theiler lifts the broken roving, and does the repairing with her thin and lovely hands. Just twists. Just gently twists.

Shows Peggy what she does and how she does it. There are lines and lines and lines, hundreds of bobbins on their spindles, spinning.

"You try," Miss Theiler says, when she spies another bit of fray. And Peggy does, Miss Theiler walking with her toward the retreating mule and calling out what to do, which isn't hard, Peggy finds. It's frankly satisfying.

Like going fishing, Peggy thinks, remembering a May day by the river with Harry and Jennie, after the boy was gone and they were doing what they could to fix Peggy's deepest missing. Jennie, sitting pretty in a new dress she'd cut out of an old dress, sat admiring the yarn on Peggy's wrist. "Looks good on you," Jennie had said, eating the last of her plum-preserve sandwich then turning her face to the sun while Harry untangled fishing line, yanked a worm from the soft clay banks, and hooked it into the end of his line. He'd kept his finger on the string, measuring tension. Only the current went by. Only the current would go by, thanks to the upstream muck that had stopped most fish from swimming. But Harry had tried, and as Harry tried, Jennie bathed her face with sun and Peggy read to them.

Now catching sight of fray on the line, Peggy reaches in. Miss Theiler puts her hand over Peggy's, to get the twisting right. No daydreaming, Miss Theiler said. No dreaming of any kind.

"Wool is a cylinder," Miss Theiler says, spying another bit of fray and walking with Peggy as Peggy twists. "A strand of wool, straight off the sheep, shall not be confused with the hair on your head. Wool is scales wrapping a hollow core. It's its own God givens that make all the making work. All of this," Miss Theiler sweeps her hand toward the floor, across the noise, beyond the stampede of the mules, the other girls working other mules, "is in the service of what wool, by its own God givens, is."

"Midwifing," she repeats, and Peggy thinks again of all that she will tell Lani, how she'll turn it into a story worth waiting for, worth living for, even. "I can help you," Peggy'd said to Lani, and she'd meant it. She could set aside some coins each week, just for Lani's baby.

"You could name her for me," Peggy'd said and Lani'd laughed, the very first laugh since before the late afternoon when she'd come to Peggy bleeding.

"That's it," Peggy hears Miss Theiler say. "That's fine. If you have questions, then you come look for me."

At lunch,

Peggy pulls her pail from her locker in the Ladies' and rides with it to the sixth floor, brushing the roving from her hair before the doors to the elevator open.

And shut.

The cab of the elevator jolts. Her stomach turns. She stands up straight like her Ma would want her to. "You represent the Finleys," her Ma had said, "wherever you decide to go."

The doors of the elevator open.

Decide.

There's a crooked line of people hoping for Fleisher's employment crowding Mrs. Velma Martine's office door—people like she'd been, but she's not those people anymore. It's a long stretch of the imagination, she discovers, to see herself in the ways that other people might be suddenly seeing her: a yarn girl straight from Fleisher's, a Balling Department doffer. New to the job. Getting the hang of it. Miss Theiler said she was getting the hang.

"You'll be needing to pick up speed," Miss Theiler had said, "but the machine likes you."

A line she'll write to the boy and address to Camp Meade. Stuff a little fluff in with the letter so that he can see for himself where she is—not with the worsteds, but still.

She runs a quick tab in her mind of the classes she is missing at High, of the gossip that will go on without her, of Mrs. Rains, fixing the bow in the scarf that she wears loose around her neck, the silk streamers flapping behind her as she walks, end of the school day, down the hall. But the day's not over. It's only just after noon. Mrs. Rains is standing at the chalkboard, stacking two dead presidents against one another, and putting out contrasting questions. Waiting for someone who isn't Peggy to dare to raise their hand.

"But what if he doesn't," she'd said about her husband, to Peggy, "come home?"

And they'd both just sat in the last branch of afternoon sun falling through the classroom window, the day's chalk settled on the floor, somebody else's footsteps passing by the door. There are questions without answers, when the history's not been made. Even then, more questions.

In the vast gleam of the dining room Peggy chooses a corner chair at a community table and thinks of the boy at Horn & Hardart spending the last of his four nickels to buy her another cup of brew. "Look," he'd said, as if she hadn't looked the first three times when the coffee streamed through the silver dolphin's nose and then the milk streamed in, afterwards and behind, warm and direct in its appeal. Every engineering miracle belonging to the boy, because he always knew, after figuring on it, the science of how, the way the one thing was inexorable with the next, if the gears were well and properly acquainted. He said things like that. She listened.

She has her pail, and she'll eat proper, and the room gets colored in— louder and louder. The men in suits or machine-grease hands, and the girls with bits of fluff in their hair, and the women like Mrs. Velma Martine, who might as well sit for one of the portraits that hang on the sixth-floor walls. They could color her purple, they could color her green, and still what a portrait she'd pose.

The boys, too, coming in with their pants too short and their bodies not tall enough for the rules, which say all workers must be at least the age of fourteen. The supervisors and the bosses. Peggy tries to guess which is whom, peeling the hard boil off the egg that she's pulled from her pail, lining up the limpy carrots, three of them, to eat in measured fashion. Wishes for some water. A square of Whitman's. She has the last of the Little Libraries in her pocket, and even though she's read this one a dozen times before, she slips it out to read it again, still a girl who loves to read. She won't stop on that, she told Ma. She'll read Guy de Maupassant until she can tell his stories in the dark to anyone who's listening.

More and more the room shades in, the talk against the porcelain clatter, the silver spoons in the bowls of soup, and now the girl with the red hair and the blue-and-star bandana takes the seat in front of her.

"Mind?"

Peggy lifts her shoulders.

"You're new," the girl says. "Saw you earlier. Getting the dilly treatment from Miss Theiler. She likes you."

"Likes me?"

The girl nods. "You can always tell."

"First day," says Peggy.

"Everybody's got to have one," the girl says. "Tomorrow will be your second, and after that you'll maintain the ordinary."

Peggy laughs.

"I'm Scoops," the girl says.

"Don't believe her," another girl says, taking the seat on the redhead's right side, shoving Peggy's pail out of the way so she might lay out a pale-blue napkin for her spread. Nice cloth. Initials on it. "So it don't get lost," the girl explains, when she sees Peggy eying the initial yellow threads. P. D. Peggy guesses she's an immigrant Londoner from the way she says her o's and i's.

"Her Christian name," the new girl jabs her spoon in Scoops's direction, "is Mary Gilroy. Family's so big it almost ran out of names. That's how she ended up with Mary."

"Didn't end up with Mary," Scoops says, smiling as she chews. Liverwurst. The smell of it filling their tip of the room.

"Thinks she's good at first base," the P. D. girl says. "Thinks she's good at everything."

"I'm an advocate for the truth," Scoops declares, using the back of her hand to swipe her mouth clean of crumbs. "And she's Pearl Dunlop," she says, introducing her friend. "Now that's a name for you."

"Better than Scoops," Pearl says, and then, to Peggy, "Got a pencil?"

"What for?" Peggy asks, rooting around in her sweater pocket as if she might have one jostling along beside the feathers. There's only the additional empty space where the Little Library was, and which she slips back to its carrying place now, before either one can ask her about it, but they'll not ask her about it, they are first-class, major-league gabbers.

"Limericks," Scoops says. "Pearl here is our resident award-winning last-line limerick writer."

"I will be," Pearl says. "One day. Awarding takes practice."

"Miss Theiler mention it, Peggy?" Scoop asks, when Peggy's mouth is full of yolk. Dry yolk. Might as well be chalk. She wishes she had water.

Peggy shakes her head.

"The Fleisher's limerick contest. Once a year. One hundred dollars to the winner."

"For a last line?" Peggy says.

"Last line's the hardest," Pearl says. "What's your name, anyhow?"

"Peggy," Peggy says. "Finley."

"Fin," Scoops says to Pearl. "Fin'll do it, don't you think?" She makes a show of sizing up Peggy.

"Duck soup," Pearl says.

"Duck soup," Scoops agrees. "Fin. Got some sheen to it. You play much ball, Peggy?"

Pearl stands and makes a swishing procession up and down beside the table, which is noisy now, a practical palaver of conversational clatter. Up and down Pearl goes, asking for a pencil, like she does every day, like they're used to it—waving her away with the back of their hands like she's a bumble that got in through the window.

"We like reading about it," Peggy answers Scoops. "Pops and I, in the newspaper."

"How are you at catch?" Scoops asks.

"Never played it."

Scoops shrugs. "Practice is after work. Games are on Sundays."

"Outfield," Scoops tells Pearl, when she comes back with a pencil in one fist. She points across the table toward Peggy. Pearl gives Peggy the once-and-thorough, then folds her dainty lunchtime napkin up and out of the way. Sets down a book of folded scraps. She leans into it with the fat nub of her borrowed pencil.

"Mashing the rhymes," she says. "Pushing past the rinky-dink."

"Don't you think?" Scoops pushes.

"Sure," Pearl says. "Outfield."

"What word you rhyming with?" Peggy asks Pearl, which is preferable, she thinks, to answering Scoops about the outfield.

"Posh," Pearl says. "Word of the day is posh." Pearl has dark-brown hair that sits on her head like a well-worn cap, the bangs sweeping over to one side and getting caught with the fringe of her lashes.

"Gosh," Peggy says, and Scoops laughs. "Good one, Fin," she says. She takes a look at Pearl's pencil work, then leans across the table, bends an eyebrow. "Bloomers," she says. "Girl ball. I'm the captain and first base, good with the glove. Pearl plays third. She pitches, too. You're centerfield. Hardly any balls get out that far."

A bell rings and Scoops and Pearl push back, stand like the business is done. "Field's across the street," Scoops says. "Practice starts straight off of work."

Still in her bed, in her room, and

the cat across the street growing familiar with its mew. The wallop reverb of the ball on the macadam jouncing up from the park, across the alley, through the walls, down the hall. Nothing in the category of shoe whisk, tap splash, or kettle song puckering the rooms below.

She was the one who bought this house, she thinks now. She was the one whose name appeared, typed, in the Agreement of Sale, made this Thirteenth day of June A.D. 1942, witnesseth that Jules Levitt, Inc. hereby agree to sell to Margaret D'Imperio, wife of Daniel D'Imperio (6841 Guyer Street) who agrees to purchase premises 6840 Guyer Street, Philadelphia, for the sum of Thirty-three hundred and ninety ——————— Dollars.

The letters of her scripted first name on the dotted signature line leaning slightly to the right and the letters of her scripted last name sitting upright on the line, except for the I of D'Imperio which tips to the left, as if it might fall to the opposite side; she remembers the weight of the pen in her hand. This will be his house, boundlessly, when she's gone—the bright molecules of air ricocheting across the open rooms and only nighttime darkness. It will be a house in which the smell of a split lemon will rollick itself out of the kitchen and up the stairs and through the open door to the room where she's been lying, but now the furniture has been rearranged, and the silver mirror and the silver brush have been vamoosed, the clink of the sun on them already dissipated, and her whole life soon departed.

It will be as if she had not lived her own story. As if the *wasn't* of her was more alive than the *was* she used to be.

Still is.

He's been out running errands an inconceivable length of time. She wonders what tricks he's taken to guarantee his delay. *Milk.* Who he's sitting with, talking to, as the hours go by, as her cancer lives on, afraid of dying.

Just lean into it, she thinks. Lean in. Let go. Murder the cancer.

As if she could tell her body what to do, or her mind, on its rounding carousel of a year in the life of her story. Two years, sometimes.

Betty—

she calls out, in the voice that's yet her own belonging, and the house apprehends. Not the girl, however, who is out in her sphere of the suburbs, where she is just now competing with her brother for the best costume of the parading season, though of course her brother will win, he always wins the important contests. In just a few days, at the end of this month, the girl will join her brother in the Halloween dark as he careens the neighborhood wearing a washing-machine box that he, with tubs of primary colors, painted. He's cut slots into his box, brushed out instructions to the candy givers with fluorescents: *Ask me a math question.* At any door upon which they knock, someone will be asked to ask the girl's brother any arithmetical at all, and beside the girl the brother will stand, performing his calculations, no pad of paper needed. He will produce the sum, the quotient, the exponential with the machinating help of the robot voice he's been rehearsing, his lips making an O that nobody will see, his cheeks pulling taut over his vowel sounds. While the girl stands there dressed as Raggedy Ann. And not even with any conviction.

The brother's bag will be rewarded with more candy than hers, and the best bars—the Butterfingers, the Clarks. She'll get the Three Musketeers, which make her choke, and the Hershey's without the almonds, and arrive home feeling empty-handed. Also stupid and too young in her Raggedy Ann, which was not a very clever costume.

None of which needs to be. All of which could be prevented, if the father would just strap the girl into his front passenger seat and drive the girl into the city, amuse himself while driving with the singing of his sillies. Leave the girl with her. Come back later.

Because the girl would like Scoops, would like Pearl, now wouldn't she? She'd like the story of the first day of Fleisher's, and how the story is the proving that, even inside the squeezing of the worst year history will ever be, which is the year of 1918, there's something you might as well chuckle over, or save up for someday telling. The girl would be preoccupied with listening, she thinks, smiles as she thinks it. She'd get that look in the brown freckles of her mostly hazel eyes when she'd come to understand how her grandmother, who'd never played catch in her life and didn't even like Jacks, came to play on a Girls team called

— Bloomers.

And then the story would go on, as she went on, carrying the girl back in time, to the middle of South Twenty-third, as she stands there practicing pitch-and-catch with Harry in the streets at dusk, roping Hannah in to race down the lost ball—all until Ma hurries them in for supper. There's Lani in the window, calling balls and strikes as if she knows a one thing. Pops sitting on the stoop, collecting the pink of the falling sky in the lenses of his glasses. Sweating.

Try to picture it, she'd tell the girl. Try to picture Scoops Mary Gilroy in her blue-and-star bandana, now already one of Peggy's dearest friends, even though she is only fourteen to Peggy's sixteen and had lied about her age two years before to get a job at Fleisher's. One of eleven. Her house the size and shape of Peggy's, and just a few blocks down on the same Twenty-third, which is an honest fact of the matter, not a story twist for a novel in memoir, a Philadelphia story, but a strange coincidence the granddaughter will come upon, years on, after finding news of Scoops and Pearl in the newspapers. The granddaughter will be the one who is entirely certain that Scoops and Pearl are Peggy (Fin) Finley's friends, or why shouldn't they be, why can't the granddaughter give this gift to her grandmother?

What harm is done?

Fin. Another name to go by.

Though Scoops would have to wait until she was "a mother of seven, grandmother of 20, great-grandmother of almost 23" to get her feature story. She would have to wait until the *Philadelphia Daily News* reporter was ready for her commentary to get her hallmark fame: "I still have the spike marks from people running into me," she'd tell the reporter, and the paper would run it, under the banner:

She hustled the bases way before others.

"I didn't care, though," she continued. "I loved to win. I was a pretty tough kid. I wasn't afraid of anything."

Pearl, for her part, got her stardom moment in medias res, after many a try at the last line of the limericks she polished. She got her fame just a few years after the year that was the worst year of all, finally winning her contest:

"Hoodoo" Limerick No. 13 Is Won by Moylan Girl | Miss Pearl Dunlop Does Not Think There Is Anything Unlucky in Much-Abused Number and Proves it | Jury of the Fleisher Yarn Mill Employee Awards Prize of ONE HUNDRED DOLLARS for Her Best Last Line

Mary Gilroy, also known as Scoops, a runner-up to Pearl Dunlop's win. It's right there, in the paper, along with her address.

Easy now.

Easy.

"Tall enough to lie." That's Scoops talking, at a Sunday doubleheader in mid-June, along the third-base sideline, the Bloomers at bat, a little momentary pause in the action. She's telling Peggy the story of her job-getting at Fleisher's, while Pearl, beside her, works out her limericks on a new pad of folded scraps and dusts Scoops's tale with a bit of her wry.

"Saw the muscles in her," Pearl says.

"Saw the look in my eye," Scoops says.

It's batter up. Pop-up. Out. It's batter up. Long fly ball right into the glove of the right fielder. Two outs. It's batter up and the bat cracks the ball, and now there's a Bloomers girl on first, and Scoops quits her storytelling, steps closer to the chalk line, touches the bill of her cap then the bend in her left elbow, and the girl, I'll call her Lorraine, sees, she knows the sign; Scoops has called a steal. Lorraine has one long lovely ponytail, her hair flowing like the groomed tail of a best-loved horse down her back. She nods. She's read the sign. Conditions being right, she's set for stealing. Just like they practiced, on Wednesdays, Scoops running the drill of her five signs.

The clouds in the sky all cool and fluffy.

The game tied at nothing nothing.

Bottom of the third.

Scoops in full-on captain mode.

Now it's Pearl's turn to take the bat. She stuffs the black fringe of her hair back into her cap so that she can see the ball that's coming. Waits for a ball to ride by. Over the plate. A strike. Another pitch, way to the outside. A strike. The count is one ball, two strikes, two outs. Scoops yells out her encouragement, and Pearl shifts her stance, spreading her two spike shoes a little farther out than shoulder width and going a bit more supple in the knees.

"That's it," Scoops yells. "That's it. You've got it."

The pitcher in her green jersey on the roughed-out mound takes a hard look at Scoops, then shakes her head at the catcher's signs. Now she throws. The ball sails in, a perfect piece of ball across the plate, which Pearl slaps mighty with her bat. It's a ground-ball beauty that takes a skip across the field to the one side of the pitcher then sneaks past the open glove of the short stop, into center.

Lorraine, already priming her steal has, all this time, been running. Rounding second base, rounding third, and when the center fielder tosses the ball to the first basewoman and it falls short, Pearl is off running, too, following Lorraine's long blond ponytail around second, now around third, where she stops. Lorraine already safely home.

The cheering is like nothing you've ever heard, and now it's Peggy's turn. Scoops smacks her on the back. She whispers in her ear. Peggy heads toward home plate to collect the bat then stands there like Scoops and Pearl and Harry, too, have taught her. The winged things in Peggy's stomach are so fruitful and multiplying that she feels their tickle all the way up in her esophagus, and then on the back of her tongue.

Peggy's cap is a little enormous for her head. She stands to fix it, then again she crouches, creases a little harder at the waist.

Leans in,

into her time, into her wedge of Girl Ball glory, there is no other way to write this, why disappoint this moment in the worst year there ever was?

Because when the ball gets thrown, when Peggy sees it coming, she swings on the nice and level and true, her bat stopping the cork-core ball from whizzing past, into the catcher's hands. The ball she has struck goes flying. She drops the bat and sees it sail. Stands there watching the ball kiss the underbelly of the sky and then she hears Scoops screaming, she hears the Fleisher's side of the crowd screaming, she runs like lightning toward first base, beating the toss, which has been thrown over the head of that poor and frustrated first basewoman. So that Pearl sees the opportunity and flies, and Peggy now takes second base, and the Bloomers are building their comfortable lead, and the Fleishers are all on their feet.

It's okay that the next batter loops a delicate fly ball off her bat and leaves Peggy stranded at second. It's just fine, because no Bloomer or friend to a Bloomer could leave this bottom of the third with disappointment. The teams switch sides on the field. Scoops trots out to first and Peggy trots out to center, and Pearl takes the mound where she belongs because Pearl is best at this and tosses the batter from the other team a nice, clean pitch, then another, and the ump calls *strike, strike, strike*, until the other team comes up short in every direction. And quick.

There's nothing doing out in center, thanks to Pearl being on the mound delivering her pitches one by one, methodical, like they're the last zinging line in a gutsy limerick, the absolute end of a story. There's nothing for Peggy to do but stand with dipped knees beneath the puffy sky and look out past the chalk lines to the crowd. To Harry, at the fence, and Pops beside him, the underarm parts of Pops's shirt sweating. To Miss Anne Theiler beside Ma, Miss Theiler's hair loose around her neck and her skirt too long for the season. And now Pearl sees who she didn't see before, when the visiting team was up at bat in the first three innings— Mrs. Rains, her silk scarf tied right, its yellow streamers streaming. Mrs. Rains, who's waving, when she sees Peggy seeing, because she has come to the Sunday Girl Ball game, because she is cheering the Bloomers on, its brand-new center fielder, because I have no choice but to write this scene the way I've put it here. For Peggy's sake. Who on this day was known as Fin. The best day in the worst year there is.

Keep the camera where it is. Don't judge. Don't call me sentimental. Give Peggy what she deserves, which is an afternoon of glory.

Pogey Bait

The doughboys who go by half their names call it your pogey bait, turning the idea of the words into a chorus: *Oh, Look here, Private Pogey Bait, would that be your munch time coming? Oh, Look here, Private Pogey Bait, popping it in, is it delicious?*

You're used to it now. Your face has changed with the smirk you've taught yourself, your expression like a shoulder shrug, your one cheek higher than the other, your upper lip pressing down toward the bottom, pulling a partial shade over the split between your teeth. You don't care what they think about you and your book: *The Pennsylvania Museum and School of Industry, Circular of the Philadelphia Textile School, Broad and Pine Streets.* (You think the whole title in your head. You do not abbreviate. Ever.) Plenty of boys lying inches away are just as steeped inside their magazines and Bibles, the recipes that their wives or mothers or sisters send along, to remind them of the taste of home. *Such a party we'll be having when you're home.* Some of the privates are writing books instead of reading them, or so it seems, with all the pencil scratching, and so who cares, or at least you don't, what they accuse you of.

The two rooms in which the practical work of woolen yarn manufacture is carried on are most admirably laid out for the purpose intended,

the book says. Words you could recite in the first hour before dawn when you're still half asleep and called for training.

One of the rooms is devoted to the dusting, burr extracting and mixing of the wools, which is accomplished by the use of the Win. Schofield improved willow, the C. C. Sargent's burr picker and the Wm. Schofield mixing picker. The other room is devoted to carding, spinning, twisting and reeling. The machinery employed consists of two sets of cards, one 48-inch Furbush, and the other 60-inch Gessner, both equipped with the latest-improved feeds 35 of the Apperly and Bramwell make; two small Torrance sampling cards for the making of fancy mixes; a 400-spindle self-acting mule, Piatt pattern, Furbush make; floor and traverse grinders, Furbush and Roy make.

Used to be that nothing to you was so lovely as a Proper Noun or a feisty stalk of rhubarb, strawberries two shades past pink, the notes that rise between the notes inside a morning bugle song, and then there she was, taller than most girls and not ashamed of it, no look of the rush to her in the pandemonium of the Saturday market. Standing there. Wanting to talk to you. Having something to say when you didn't, something to laugh at that you couldn't have guessed was funny, though now you can. You can see her funny coming.

And her letters, arriving erratic at the base P.O., which you have to hitch your ride to, one way or the other. Every single one of those letters saying the surprising. Explaining: Negotiations with her teachers. Pops leaving without his lunch pail. Twice. Something worrying on Lani. Mrs. Velma Martine. Miss Anne Theiler. The Bloomer girls of Fleisher's. The mules and the carders and the combers of Fleisher's. The puffs of frayed yarn blowing upward like backwards confetti, then wafting down, into her hair, onto her shoulders, inside her pockets, and how, when she walks home through the streets she hears the knitting needles being plucky, the miles and miles and miles of Fleisher's yarn making what the doughboys'll need, in the doughboy colors. For the trenches. For the battles coming.

And birds, she writes, overhead, are flying. And there's more feathers in her pocket, and William Shakespeare's sonnets, and:

The city is yarn, she writes. *Uncountable miles of doughboy khaki and the clack of gauged metal needles. The sound of the yarn is on the stoops, on the other side of open windows, on the street corners where women stand, the hanks of it in their baskets, their hands moving fast beneath their aggravated worry.*

Peggy writes it so that you can see it, so that you are never as far away from her as Meade is far away from Philadelphia. You imagine her sitting on the top stone by her front door, doing the writing on the thin paper she has bought from McDougal's Corner Store, or taking whatever part of the lunchtime table Pearl doesn't need for her embroidered napkin or her last-line notebook.

You can't imagine, Peggy writes, *Pearl's tuck of lines.*

It's Peggy's letters that you've stashed inside the *Circular of the Phila-delphia Textile School*. Peggy's letters that you read now, instead of the bound-in pages, while the other privates with half their names think you're dreaming worsted again.

Truth is, the worsted's fading. Truth is, you've put to memory something you're not sure you'll ever have a working need for; you've admired machines that maybe, now, will always be purely theoretical in their ways and means. Boys like you are dying over there. They're coming home in caskets. You see it in the news the privates of the 314th Infantry Regiment, 79th Division are reading, in the gray light of yesterday's papers, in the barracks, in the log-cabin headquarters, in the line at the P.O.

Don't think on it. Don't dwell. Appreciate the fine murine inside your pocket. The white and gray coat, good as worsted, and the pale-pink nose and the serrated whiskers that you espied down by the stables, when you were off the clock and you thought you'd give some comfort to the wild-eyed Quarter Horses that'll be shipped, on a day that's coming soon, right out to war beside you.

The horses need more metal shoes than the army has supplies for. They need bridles but are only dressed in those thin halters. They need more feed than the local farmers can haul, more than the twenty-five acres they've been given in this part of Anne Arundel County, where there's, what? thousands of buildings across the cantonment, in addition to the horses.

You gave a salute to Major Peter F. Meade at Remount 304 on the day you found the mouse. You stood there, in your uniform, on the far edge of the stable, standing straight as you'd been instructed, feeling a scurry between your ankle and your knee beneath the thin cloth of your trousers.

Waited for the Major to pass.

Bent at your waist once he did.

Saw the zigzag of the thing trapped in the dark side of your pant leg. Felt, even more, the rambunctious tickle of it.

You had a heel of Schmidt's Crusty in the empty well of your uniform. You stuffed your fist in, broke a piece off, crouched down and slid your trouser leg up slowly, by the hem. You only saw the tail at first, the soft bone and new nerves of a baby rodent searching, you guessed, for its mother.

You were gentle, and you pulled. You held the blinking squirm of the baby murine upside down by its tail for only that one second, then placed its scratchy four paws on your open palm. You sprinkled some crumbs of Crusty's down, and the paws went from crazy to calm. You sprinkled more crumbs, and you sprinkled some more, until the mouse trusted the map of your hand.

The horses in the stables braying. The sound of other privates far off at Meade, digging their own trenches, drilling with their gas masks on, whistling to the Hello Girls come to visit, who shushed them with the mystery of their exotic French words.

By the time you were back at the barracks, the mouse had a name. It was Crumbs.

The mouse had a home. In your pocket.

The other privates got along with the idea; only one or two protested. Saving crumbs for Crumbs became a thing you all did, calling you by your best tag—*Look here, Pogey Bait*—whenever they wanted a turn with the mouse, which you'd encourage from your pocket. Whiskers brimming over the rim of your pocket, then the pale tip of the nose coming up, then the eyes, black as poppy seeds when the light hit them soft, creating a confusion of reflections.

"Be careful," you'd say, but you didn't have to, these men of war so spontaneously gentle that it is the first thing you'll tell Peggy, when you write her your next letter, it being June now, with the command come in that you'll be leaving for Hoboken in a few weeks' time, and from Hoboken you'll be leaving for the war, which is across the seas, where so many men are dying.

So you read her letters, folded neat inside the *Circular*. So you leave Crumbs to run up and down the short posts of your bed; he'll go no further. You take on Scoops in your imagination, and the stampede of Miss Anne Theiler's self-acting mules, and Pearl at lunch with her borrowed pencil. It turns out that Fleisher's Yarns is more about people and less about machines, which is not something you'd have guessed when you stood on the corner of Twenty-sixth and Reed with Peggy at your side and watched the building gain its height and broad-faced windows. Not something you'd ever read in the *Circular*, because it wasn't something that was written for the pages you had thought contained your future.

It's something that Peggy writes, in her letters. Something that rides your bones, by the way of her telling—the talk of the machines, the velocity of spin, the rumble of the bobbin carts, up and down the endless rows. There's no talking back to the machines, Peggy writes, saying there's no shushing them either, even after she leaves and heads home, to South Twenty-third, walking the dusk hour alongside Scoops now, who plans the roster for the next Bloomers game or tells impossible pinochle stories or names all ten of her brothers and her sisters, then tells Peggy to name hers.

Scoops talks, but it's the throttling clangor of the machines that Peggy hears, the thrum and roar that she carries. The idea she has—she wrote it in a letter—that the making of yarn is the next thing past human, that it enters your blood, and it breathes.

Home now,

she opens the door and closes it behind her. Unlaces her high-tops. Leaves them by the door. Hears the sound of music scratching over the boom-echo of machines in her ears, and there's Ma and Lani and now there's Harry leaning against the wallpapered wall, where the seam has come undone and the chipped-paint with plaster beneath shows itself to be lilac hued.

Lani's dark hair has come loose from its Gibson Girl pins. There's more room in her face than there used to be, her mouth and her nose having stretched out, wider. She's wearing a high-necked, wide-girthed tunic with plenty of extra to it. She's wearing her old, scuffed worn-in shoes. How she got here, Peggy cannot guess—who dug her out of the cave of her room with what kind of shovel or spoon. Who walked her down her own steps, through her own door, and across the street and up the stoop, but she's here, some ribbon of joy running through as Ma sings along with the ridiculous song that spins beneath the needle of the Victrola.

Harry coming in on the verse.

And now Johnny's wed and he wished that he were dead,

And they all had a finger in the pie.

Poor fool, they all had a finger in the pie.

Ma reaches her hand toward Peggy. "Your dinner's warming," she says, kissing Peggy on the cheek as if Peggy's finally full forgiven. Harry lifts the needle up and puts it back down on the place where the song begins. He makes like Peggy hasn't missed a thing. The American Quartet is singing.

If you would be single and of marriage you're afraid,

Never mingle in a home where there's a shy old maid.

The song has a good military marching beat, a tempo no one in their patriotic mind would deny, and now, one hand on Peggy's shoulder and one hand at Peggy's hip, Ma carries the tune off in a circular galumph, drawing Peggy with her around the brief circumference of the room. Tipping the lamp Harry yanks out of their way. Bruising the faded yellow cotton hem of the apron tied around Ma's waist. Against the clawed feet of the stuffed couch, they smudge and brush. Against the walnut bureau. Against the peeling places of the wallpaper. Careful near the Victrola.

Ma and Harry sing the song out to its end; anyone on the street could hear it. Good thing Jennie's not home, or Sarah either, the others. Good thing Pops is still at the Arsenal, doing the end of his double shift. The tufts of roving that had flecked inside Peggy's curls from her day at Fleisher's shake themselves loose and fly. They float like doughboy-colored clouds above them.

Wisps.

"Ma," Peggy says, laughing now, out of breath, but Ma has plenty more song in her. Harry lifts the needle and puts it down again. He trades places with Peggy and Ma spins him, even though he is the taller one by at least a long forearm and twice Ma's dancing strength. Peggy feels the spin in her head. She leans against the part of the wall where Lani's been standing all this while and waits for an explanation.

"Came to find you," Lani says. "To tell you first."

Peggy tries to picture that—Lani digging her own self out of bed, walking her own self across the street, pinning her hair back with nervous fingers until Ma opened the door. Or maybe Jennie. Peggy's pleaded with Lani, all this while. She's brought her pansies and yarn fluff, news from the boy, news of the world, a Sampler, even, but nothing in all this time has budged Lani, except for here, boasting of her own volition, she is.

Lani lifts Peggy's hand to place it just below her waist. Peggy sees, in that moment, the true nature of the dress, it being one of Ma's old dresses, only with a new lace collar sewn in, Irish lace, and a silk orange ribbon woven into the cuff of the right wrist. Peggy wonders if Lani spent the whole day here. If Ma was given the new news first, because Peggy wasn't here, because Peggy's just another working girl inside the maw of the machining at Fleisher's.

"Feel it?" Lani asks.

Peggy applies more pressure with her resting hand. She closes her eyes and narrows every thought until she feels the surface of her palm prick.

"She's kicking," Lani says. Her loose hair nearly tangled up with Peggy's, she doesn't have to shout.

"Oh yes," Peggy says, startled now, for there again it is: the Morse code of a baby's foot. One strike. Then two.

"She's pretty, don't you think?" Lani says, tears in her eyes as she says it.

"Oh yes," Peggy says. "Pretty as you." And Peggy thinks of the jar upstairs where she's been stashing her spare Fleisher's coins, the baby jar, is what she calls it. "You'll be all right," Peggy'd been telling Lani all this time, up in Lani's bedroom above the widowed Mrs. who, if she knew by now, and how could she not, was neither scolding Lani nor helping. Peggy going in and out, up and down, telling Fleisher's stories, Bloomer stories. Peggy bringing some of Ma's home-cookeds to Lani in a silver pail, or a wooden box of berries from the market.

And all this time, Lani in the sour bed in the same drab dress, her job at Whitman's gone to someone else, the chocolate running over the coconut centers under the care and guidance of another, until, at last, she wasn't talking pennyroyal, begging Peggy to go out and find it, or turpentine will do, just ask George Furloin.

"I will not," Peggy had said, and for a while there was no trust between them.

And now, here, Lani is, her hair falling down while Ma and Harry flounce to the kind of song that makes trouble seem like it could never come knocking at the door again. Like all the trouble is behind them. In the middle of the war. In the worst year there'd ever be.

He's married now

He don't know how

And when and where or why

"She's all mine," Lani says, meaning the baby, Peggy guesses.

"Of course she is."

"And yours," she says, "if that'd be fine with you, would it be, Peggy?"

"Aunt Peggy," Peggy says. "Will spoil your baby rotten."

She hears the door open

and close behind her husband, a patter across the house, a rustle in the kitchen. There's the sweet suck of the refrigerator door, a grocery-store bag tossed into the silver canister he operates with the dainty tip of his size 9 Aristocraft oxfords, which will be newly polished. Don't go anywhere, he's always said, without your leathers polished.

She waits for him to settle into his parlor chair, in the room beneath hers, to snap the TV on. Maybe the Eagles are playing, and the squad has possession of the ball, is running it downfield, toward the touchdown line, at Franklin Field. She concentrates. Gives herself over to very air itself, gauges its tremble, loses herself within the stretch of her own senses. If there are crowds in the arena far away she cannot hear them. Perhaps the wind is blowing the other way. Perhaps there's wind?

Peg? She hears her name from close by now, her husband's knuckles on her door. She hears the ice chime inside one of those tall, narrow glasses, feels his weight on the side of her bed. His corporation.

Lemons were on sale, he says. *And oranges.*

All her strength to gain an angle in the bed. All her imagination to imagine him climbing the stairs with this glass in hand, stopping as he often did, mid-transit, before the painting of the pigtailed girl on the stairway wall. The lucky painting, they called it, because that was the one she'd brought home from a flea-market fair, certain there was more to it than a girl with two braids and a floppy hat on her head. She'd taken the sharpest kitchen knife to the brown-paper backing and sliced through, and there it was, like criminal loot, a fistful of bills—fives and tens and twenties, one Benjamin Franklin, too.

They threw the money in the air. They danced. The Charleston swivel, she remembers now. Beside her husband and her son, her daughter being off with her best friend Carol, missing all the fun.

He's split a half-slice of orange over the rim of the glass, made sure to keep the seeds out. He tells her it will do her some good, and it does, her mouth so parched.

Brought you something, he says now, and she realizes that he's been sitting there with that book of pictures in his hand. The book of the day of their daughter's marriage to that handsome engineering man.

He helps scoot her over toward the middle of her bed, which was their bed once, and for a long time. Holds her glass of fresh squeezed until she finds her angle again. He sits beside her, bends his knees, and props the white naugahyde album so that she can see it. Enough daylight in the room for this. Enough room in the bed, which has been so lonely. She adjusts her angle to the fresh slope in the bed, and he opens the book, turns the first crinkle of the pages. A slight smell of mold comes up out of time.

There she is, the girl's mother, sublime. Caught in the reflective glass of her bedroom window, a wallpaper garden around her. She is perfectly fit into her high-necked princess gown, its pair of lace sleeves drawing their fragile conclusions at her wrists, the veil falling down from her crown. The bride lifts a tube of lipstick to her lips, and though the photograph is black and white, Peg sees the gold of the tube, the red of the lip wax her daughter, the girl's mother, wore that day.

Always a beauty, her husband says, and Peg lowers her chin in agreement.

The silver hand mirror is on the bureau before the bride. A piece of Irish lace beneath the silver. Generations of women inside this single photograph.

Look at you, her husband says, turning the page, which is heavy, for each photograph has been framed in the same naugahyde as the album cover and slipped inside a sleeve of industrial-grade plastic. She struggles not to see but to remember herself like this—upright in middle age, white gloves on, a strand of pearls at her neck, a corsage of calla lilies, the cancer as of yet nothing less than a gnaw of anxiety within her. A hat plumes feathers on her head. She tries to remember now how she had come upon that hat, in what shop window she had seen it, this two-inch-tall pillbox. It looks as if a bird has landed on her head and tucked its head inside a wing. Such exuberance, to choose a hat like that, for her only daughter's wedding day.

Now us, her husband says, turning to another page, and there he is, in his white tuxedo jacket and his black bow tie, flanking their daughter on her right side, while Peg stands to the daughter's left. His hair is white at the edges and Brylcreemed back. His smile isn't big enough for the day, and neither is the bride's—both of them looking as if they'd swallowed their thoughts while Peg's joy for the moment is alive. She's taller than he is. She's not embarrassed of her height. She has a mink stole looped over her left arm and a tiny boxy useless purse looped over her wrist.

The photographer of Becker Studios coaxes the three to smile again, but it's only when they open the door at 6840 Guyer and the bride gets some air beside her father at that threshold does she smile big enough for both of them, for the great salesman of Life remains wary. Sitting at this angle in her bed, sipping the fresh squeezed, tipping the juice back until the ice chimes, she studies that. Then sees herself through the window glass—flowers now in her white-gloved hands.

It startles her, how alive she was.

Let's go back, she wants to say to her husband. Let's go back and start again.

Forgive me, she wants to say. For loving, from the start, the boy. For never letting on. Or go.

Forgive me. Please.

Down the aisle at Southwestern Presbyterian. A kiss on the bride's cheek in the hall. So many curly headed children wearing angel wings and laundered collars tossing the rice confetti, but who are those children, after all? She can't remember one. She puts her hand on her husband's hand, hoping he will stop, but he continues on, turning the naugahyde pages until here, now, is her son, wearing the same white jacket and black bow tie that her husband, in the pictures, has on. He is handsome tall, his height her gift to him, his body, like hers, built for dancing, his laughter, like hers, throwing out flares, and in the pictures he is laughing.

She is, all of a sudden, warm, regardless of the ice in her glass, which has lost its musical charm. She scans the photographs for a glimpse of Lani, but of course she isn't there. She scans for Ma and Pops and Harry; she's confusing things now, she's very pale, so very tired. She feels the brush of her husband's dry lips on her forehead, hears the heavy close of the book in his hand. His creaking knees straightening. The mattress easing. The glass of fresh squeezed being taken from her hand. The door about to close.

To remember by, her husband says, and she tries to turn to get a look at him, but the past comes rushing in.

Pops

is dead. Joseph Carver, the hammerer at his side, the fitter of soles to boots at the Arsenal, has come running all this way to tell them, late in the afternoon, near toward supper time. Peggy is upstairs in Lani's house fashioning a list of sporting baby names when she hears her mother on the top stone step outside—a scream so feral Peggy knows at once what it is, knows she has to run, she can't remember running, down the stairs at Lani's, into the street, up the stoop, to catch Ma.

Jennie appearing out of nowhere now. Harry far away, at Baldwin's. The others wherever they go to, how is Peggy supposed to remember?

"No, Ma," Peggy says, as if saying a thing isn't true makes the thing not true and saves the brokenhearted.

There is no saving the brokenhearted.

Mr. Carver walks straight in. Helps Peggy and Jennie help Ma to the couch, turns off the Victrola, which had the flip side of The American Quartet playing; Ma'd been singing while Ma'd been cooking. The stew on the cookstove still steeps. In the kitchen Mr. Carver calms the coals, stirs the stewpot so its bottom won't burn, and pours a glass of coolest water from the water jar.

He returns to Ma with the glass, but Ma can't see him. Her eyes buried in Jennie's shoulder. Her hand squeezing Peggy's blinding tight. Nobody wanting Mr. Carver there because him being there just confirms what the man has said. He'd have no business being there if he had not carried news.

But Mr. Carver is doing his felt duty. He touches the part of Ma's shoulder he can reach and kneels down for some explaining.

"Oh, Ma," Jennie says. "Dear Ma." Mr. Carver continues.

Says it was a day just like any other day. Maybe the factory a little hotter than it'd been the day before. Maybe a bar of sun striping itself down heavy across Pops's shoulders. Maybe there being too many boots, always another useless doughboy boot until the sole got hammered on.

Don't know what it was that made him turn, except maybe he heard the slightest bump. A soft noise in a loud place, which was the sound of Pops sighing, Mr. Carver thought, the sound of a man wiping the sweat from his brow, and he turned to give Pops an acquiesce, a sympathizing nod. But when he turned, he saw it. Pops's face blanched and profusely sweating. One hand gripping his chest.

"Mr. Carver," Peggy interrupts, for Ma is about to die herself from hearing of Pops's dying.

"Mrs. Finley, have some water," Mr. Carver says. Mrs. Finley, Samuel Finley, man of my heart, Ma always called him, the Bainbridge Street boy she'd married and grown up with, the father of her children. Peggy's aware of the smell of leather on Mr. Carver, the same smell her father carried home from his first and second shifts then took off before supper. Pops's second pair of clean clothes always worn for Ma's supper, like he was going to church to eat at her table.

"Your boy," Ma said once, on that day at Willow Grove, as they strolled along by the lake. Ma's elbow had been crooked in hers. Harry and the boy had wandered up ahead. "He's a lot like your Pops was when I met him. Full of his respect for me. And still is," Ma said, a tug on Peggy's elbow. "Your boy's like that. Just take a look at him."

"You think I haven't looked at him?" Peggy said, and Ma had laughed, pulled her even closer.

Mr. Carver won't stop talking. He won't quit his story, feels compelled to see it through, like a newspaper man, reporting. Mr. Carver shouting for help as Pops began to teeter and fall. Mr. Carver lowering Pops to the Arsenal floor within the nick of time. Help coming. Men leaving their hammers and nails and hurrying to Pops's side, Mr. Carver holding Pops's head with the palms of his hands and another man loosening Pops's tie. They unbuttoned his shirt to help him breathe. They called out for water, some came. They called for help, but they were the help there was, until the boss made his way into the thick of the crowd, and by then it was too late. It was like Pops couldn't hear any comforts that any of them said. He couldn't hold on.

His eyes, Mr. Carver is saying, rolled back to the farthest parts of his head, and he was gone, and Mr. Carver isn't sure, because of the Arsenal noise and Pops's voice being so gone, but he feels certain saying anyway that Pops was calling for Ma in the end. That his name for Ma was the last word he said.

"Sure thing," Mr. Carver says. "Sure as I'm standing here."

They don't want him standing here.

Then the boss sent Mr. Carver running up ahead, all the way to South Twenty-third, the Finley address in his hand, and is there a funeral home, Mrs. Finley, we should call, is there arrangements we can help you be making?

"Where," Jennie asks, "is Pops now?"

"We put a clean sheet over him," Mr. Carver says, like this was his own doing. "We put him in a storage room and said for no one to touch him."

Ma nearly tumbles to the worn-out carpet. She grips her own heart over her apron with her right hand.

There'll be more men coming soon, Mr. Carver continues. There'll be the floor boss, or the superintendent, or somebody official with the Quartermaster, bringing them nothing but the news that is confirming, and maybe the last part of Pops's pay, what the government will owe him, maybe the silver pail with his part of lunch still in it, waiting for a break in the day when he might go outside and eat the pie Ma'd made just to his liking. "You're good to me, Love," he'd said, hours before this one, and it occurs to Peggy that this dying happened near about noon, because Pops had not stopped to eat his lunch, and so why had Mr. Carver come here running?

Just this morning Peggy had been looking at herself in the two rounds of his glasses. Smudge on both lenses, factory oils, something she'd have cleaned that night with the hem of her skirt, when he'd gotten home for supper, she'd have been on the lookout, would have met him halfway down the block and walked him home for supper.

Ma hunches her shoulders in, toward her chest—a woman protecting the soft parts of her heart from losing the man that she loves. With the flesh of her chest, with the bones of her ribs, she will not let Pops depart, will not abide the news that Mr. Carver brings. She clenches Peggy's hand so hard inside her own that Peggy thinks she hears her fingers crunch, but that's the sound that Ma's heart is making.

Somebody has to tell Harry, bring him home. Ma won't right survive this if Harry isn't coming.

"I'll go for Harry," Peggy hears herself say, though Baldwin's is far on the other side of the city, and she can't run that far, but she will.

Putting Ma's hand in Jennie's hand. Leaving Ma's face still buried in Jennie's shoulders. Leaving Mr. Carver standing there with the untouched glass of water in his hand, his hat still on, his oats-colored cotton collar amber with the sweat that doesn't come off in anybody's wash.

"Fast as I can, Ma, I promise," Peggy says, and when she straightens up and dries her face and clears her eyes of the tears that still are coming, she sees Lani in the doorway wearing the dress that Ma had made her, saying, "Is it the worst of it?"

And Peggy nods.

They leave

the house together. Lani's arm across Peggy's shoulders, tugging Peggy close when Peggy stumbles. Lani won't say *there, there*, because she knows which words are useless, knows there are no words with any sense to them when it comes to a father dying.

Lani knows because she knows. Because her own Pa set off one day to go skating on the Schuylkill, middle of a cold snap, ice should have been a nice thick skin above the frigid current. Lani was eight when she heard her mother keen, when she understood what the story was—that her Pa was blades strapped on and sailing away from the banks and hockey players, the little-girl twirlers, the hands in his gloves in a knot at his back, when the ice opened up beneath him and the river swallowed. That it was his body that drowned in the flow beneath the ice, floating all the way toward the Delaware River, where, a week to the day when he didn't come home, at a reedy intersection of the city's two long rivers, his body was found, his hands frozen through though his gloves were still on. Just like that, Lani's Pa was vanished, and after that, her mother was mostly gone off too, into herself, nothing after that worth saying, or saying much. Lani's mother turned gray between the dawn and the dusk of a single day. She shriveled in her chair. It was Lani's father who had been the German, and a baker at that, the sugar man in a confectioner's shop, which is how Lani grew up to have the sweet tooth in her. Also the German.

She says *I'm sorry*, not *there, there*. She says *I'm so sorry, Peggy*.

Tugs her close.

Wipes off Peggy's tears, but the tears keep coming.

It's been so long now since Lani has been out walking. Still, she knows the way to Baldwin's, or at least the streets to take toward the general locale of the dozens of buildings on seventeen acres that stretch west from North Broad and south from Spring Garden, this being the world's top locomotive shop. Every proud Philadelphian can boast Baldwin, and Lani, no matter what those men did, no matter what words they said, is still a Philadelphian; she was never for the Kaiser. There are Baldwin men for boilers, bolts, and axles; men for welding, lathing, gears; men for day work and for night work; and a couple of Baldwin women in finely made blouses bent over Baldwin typewriters, taking dictation and orders.

That would be something, Lani thinks, to call yourself something so proper as a Baldwin woman.

Harry'll be in the finishing shop, at the corner of Broad and Spring Garden. Lani knows as much from Peggy. Doesn't know where the door is, doesn't know who the boss is, doesn't know what they will do once they arrive there. Doesn't know what they will say to convince the supervisor to go, please, please hurry, find Harry. Harry Finley. She puts it out of her mind, there are still some blocks to go, there is still Peggy, beside her, to keep upright.

She is part of this, she thinks of it now. Part of the ruining of Harry.

Harry, I'm so sorry.

North through the neighborhoods, east through the city, north again, quick to the curbs and careful near the crush of cart wheels, Fords, and trolleys, toward the smokestacks in the shortening distance, the low gray plumes of chimney exhaust that make their own stratosphere of weather. Her arm all this time across Peggy's shoulders, holding her as close as she with her widening hips and baby can, she doing the taking care, she had forgotten she could do this.

The patriots on the streets sizing up each other, and sizing Lani. The snapping of hoisted flags above their heads. The needles knitting on the stoops, inside the parlors. The smack of the ads for the Liberty Loans up against the brick and the sound of the horns and the horses.

Almost to Broad, headed to Spring Garden, the smoke in their eyes now, the weather above them changing. It's Peggy who stops then, though Lani's feeling nauseous. Peggy who says, "Lani, I can't do this."

"But you will do it, Love," Lani says. "You promised Ma that you would."

At the funeral

Ma holds Peggy's hand and Lani holds Peggy's hand and Jennie, God alone knows how she does it, stands before all the Finleys and the handful of the rest at First Presbyterian Church on Washington Square and sings The Lord Is My Shepherd, her voice so crystalline that it comes back now, after all these ruined years, the words on the stilts of the notes. No one playing the piano, no one singing below the melody, just Jennie in a white dress with a black ribbon tied around her neck, a knot Jennie finished with an undecorative bow.

He makes me down to lie

In pastures green, He leadeth me

In pastures green, He leadeth me

Harry standing behind them in the back of the near-to-empty House of the Lord because he cannot sit down for this. He's been on his feet since he'd been brought the news. He'd steadied himself against the shell of a half-built locomotive, then steadied Peggy against himself. He'd left Baldwin's soon as he was standing straight and went running all the way home, a black dash through the streets between the horses and the trolleys, ahead of Peggy and Lani. Leaving Peggy's news still beating its wings in the clangor of the finishing shop at North Broad and Spring Garden. Then Peggy and Lani blocks behind, the dusk coming in, the curtain of night soon to fall across the city.

Ma had to be gotten to. Peggy told Harry, "You go. We're here. Behind."

Lani nervous near the alleyways, but there were two of them, together, their sadness like a shield.

My soul He doth restore again,

And me to walk doth make

Peggy in the pew, watching Jennie, the prettiest Finley, sing, but seeing in her mind's eye a Sunday afternoon, not so many weeks ago when Peggy and Harry and Ma were dancing to a noisy tune and Pops came down the stairs. He wore the better of his two shirts, a new shine on his shoes, no arsenal dirt on his spectacle lenses. He crossed the room, toward the Victrola. Sifted the stash of records that were kept upright in their sleeves on a shelf above the player. Found what he was looking for. Lifted the needle on the present song and replaced it with the sad side of Manuel Romain.

The needle going down.

The roses each one

Met with the sun

Sweetheart, when I met you

"May I?" he said, to Ma. Harry and Peggy stepping back, climbing the stairs, sitting one worn step above the other, to give their parents the brief circumference of the room. Pops taking Ma into his hold and slow waltzing. Pops gentle with his wife, careful, as if she were herself a rose, as if he knew what was to come and this was the only way to tell her.

The sunshine had fled

The roses were dead

Sweetheart, when I lost you

Pops losing Ma. That's how he would have thought of it, Peggy thinks, sitting in the pew. Never imagining, for there was no more modest a man, the love they'd keep in store for him, the wide and the long of their missing him, the endless of their losing.

"Dan?"

she calls, but he's gone out again.

When she sighs, she sighs all the missing.

Him, too.

She loved the man she married. That, too, she realizes now, was practically a secret. That too cannot be fixed.

Peggy sleeps

after that in the bed beside Ma. She watches the moon catch the light in the lenses of Pops's spectacles, which Ma has placed across the room on the dresser where another woman's box of jewels might go. The moon in the glass, then the glass going dark, then the day breaking and with the breaking of the day, two small yellow flares in the lenses on the bureau. Peggy cleans the glasses every day. With the hem of her skirt. With the cuff of a sleeve. Picks them up and shines them, puts them back, just as Ma had.

Ma doesn't sleep, but when she sleeps, she calls out for Pops, and Peggy answers, cradling her mother in her arms.

"It's me, Ma. I know. I'm here."

A glass of water at the bedside for Ma to sip, if Peggy can get her up at the proper sipping angle. A book to read, a Little Library, if Ma can listen. Peggy's sweater hung over the bedpost and the feathers in its pocket held up at dawn, for her mother to see, soft proofs of the eternal.

"See how pretty, Ma."

Jennie takes a second job, this one with the honey seller down at the Reading Market, where her prettiness alone draws customers to the vendor stand like bees. Sarah takes some laundry in and lives, it seems, down in the dank and rumble of the basement. Harry works more hours, and when he comes home, so late, he isn't well. There's something slant about him.

"You were right," Ma says one morning, as Peggy packs her pail for work. "We need you now, at Fleisher's."

Scoops says it's all right to stop playing ball and it's all right to stop being Fin, but it's not all right for Peggy to go astray in her thinking while the mule stampedes and the roving twists and the spindles spin their madness. "You'll get a hand knocked up," she says, shouts it over the din, when she catches Peggy staring into space. "You'll break a knee. Machines don't stop for the daydreamers." Miss Anne Theiler is also keeping out an eye, and on the eighth day after Peggy returns to her place among the doffers, the boy with the cart that takes the bobbins away brings Peggy half an apple and cheese sandwich. "Don't need the other half," is what he says to her, shy, and Peggy wants to cry for the kindness of it, and for seeing herself as he sees her—too thin, too pale, too broken.

Late one afternoon, after the day shift has been called, it's raining. Pearl is waiting for Peggy in the Ladies' lounge, and when Peggy shows up to hang her Fleisher's apron, Pearl tells Peggy that they're going upstairs for the Wednesday concert. "Best part of the week," Pearl says, about this entertainment and education hour, slipped into the midweek schedule when Peggy was off mourning. "You're not going to miss it."

"Can't," Peggy says. "Ma'll be looking for me."

"Scoops," Pearl contradicts, "has that covered." Says that Scoops is already headed Ma's way, to give her the news on Peggy's staying late, Pearl as chaperone, so that Ma won't worry. Ma worries now about what she can't see. Ma worries when someone comes knocking. Ma will worry when she sees Scoops on the Finley stoop, her hair rivuleting rain, her boots full of squish, but Scoops will set Ma's mind at ease in the matter of an instant. Will sit with Ma, do some talking. Walk across the parlor, dripping.

"Peggy's fine," Scoops will say. "Pearl's taking care."

"I'll get you a towel," Ma will say. She'll take Scoops's long one braid apart and brush the tangles out. Put her boots by the cookstove to dry. It's good for Ma to have something to do. Something that doesn't remind her of Pops.

"Peggy's getting some music in," Scoops will say, when they're ready, and because Ma's face will still be rumpled in a rubric of worry, because

Scoops doesn't know that's who Ma has forever now become—furrowed and timid and anxious, too anxious to take a long story in—Scoops will go on to explain. How the Mr. Fleishers have started a Wednesday serenade for the yarn workers. *The* Mr. Fleishers, Scoops will emphasize. *The* Mr. Samuel Fleisher of the Graphic Sketch Club for the lesser-offs down on Catherine. *The* Mr. Edwin Fleisher of the Symphony Club, for boys and girls, Blacks and whites. The Fleishers of Fleisher's Yarn creating the Wednesday after-work hour right there, in the soar of their building at Reed. Five o'clock, take your apron off, come upstairs and have a listen. Comfortable chairs drawn into a half circle. A man at the piano, who is both the player and the singer. The popular songs and also some classics, with Miss Anne Theiler remarking in between, providing instructions on what is to be heard, and how.

"Miss Theiler?" Ma will ask. "The same one as—?" Proof that, despite all the meander of Scoops's talk, Ma has had the wherewithal to listen.

"The very same," Scoops will say. Educating the carders and combers and dyers and doffers on melody, harmony, lyrics, Scoops doesn't actually know what or which, because she's never been to a Wednesday serenade, she's just heard of it from Pearl, who says it's the third-best thing in life, alongside limericks and Bloomers. The fourth-best thing being working at Fleisher's, where Pearl is a dyer, by the way. A stink of a job, and yet she likes it.

"You're not much for music?" Ma will ask.

"Pinochle," Scoops will say. "That's my second best, to Bloomers."

Ma will be eased back in her chair by now, her face the same but her shoulders different. "It'll be good for Peggy, then," Ma says, while Peggy, already up high at Twenty-sixth and Reed, has taken a seat beside Pearl. Turning around to look over her shoulder, through the window, at the rain, which has become a worse pour.

When all the chairs have been filled and all the fray of loose yarn has settled, when the rough hands of the workers are resting on the hand-me-down skirts and overalls and trousers, Miss Theiler sweeps in, looking grandiose without her apron and with her hair piled higher on her head.

"A welcoming hand for Mr. Edgar Shore," she says, and the piano player takes his seat above the keys and lifts his lithe, suspenseful hands. He wears a doughboy-colored sweater and a magnificent pair of patched-twice trousers. Rain has come in, cool as pewter, a chill in it, though now the room is warming.

"With no further ado," Miss Theiler says, "we begin with Brahms Piano Concerto No. 2 in B-flat major, a piece Johannes Brahms created over the length of three years and dedicated to his father. We begin with an ease. We'll find ourselves in the midst of a scherzo. The piece was written for an orchestra, but the piano alone is delightful. Mr. Shore," she nods, "if you please." She lifts one arm as if directing the absent orchestra and all the extra fabric in her shirt sleeve blossoms. Then she takes her seat.

Mr. Shore lets his fingers drop, and the room itself seems to shiver. The start of the song is a tease, the fingers moving from left to right as if they are out for a Sunday stroll. But now the pace quickens. Now the fingers are proving their forcefulness, gathering so many notes at once and with alarming speed.

Pearl takes Peggy's hand. She squeezes. Peggy watches the man at the keys, the intensity with which he strikes out at the Brahms, a concerto written for a father and played by a man she recognizes now: Mr. Shore is the boss of the carders. Mr. Shore is a Fleisher like his audience is, and this is what she'd want to tell her father, this is why she'd run through the rain to the Arsenal after this, to help Pops with his pail and to walk the blocks beside him, avoiding the mud and the tail-flick of horses, the trolleys spraying by.

"A practical symphony," she'd say. "But only one man at the piano."

In the quiet parts between the louder parts, Peggy can hear the rain through the windows behind her. She hears a rumble, then sees the refracted crack of a lightning strike, brightening the room but not disturbing Mr. Shore. Miss Theiler is mesmerized beyond the weather. This, Peggy realizes, is where she does her daydreams, off the clock, in the company of music.

If only Pops could see. If only she could tell him. If only she could tell the boy what has happened to the Finleys. Pops not going to war, but dead anyway. Ma gone gray and pale, not sleeping. Jennie wasting her pretty on honey. Harry coming home too late, and tipsy.

If only she could tell the boy, but she has not written him a letter, because if she writes it down, it will become her worst true story. If she sends the words she can't write through the mail to Camp Meade, it will just be one of many manifolding hurts, riding the rails in every direction, none of them the same and all of them together.

If he could just come home. If he would hold her.

Correspondence

She doesn't tell you. Harry does. In a letter short, the words in it starting at the left side and falling to the right. Which was delivered unto you after you had stood in the swerve of the line at the P.O., Crumbs's heartbeat a patter in your pocket. All the other sergeants, waiting. The day's humidity in their uniforms. Their heads bent. Not much talk to the day, but plenty of fly buzz, the smell of the manure from Remount 304 following you all the way here, to the Post. It was your turn at the window and they had mail for you, a letter.

You had two letters of your own to send, but you stepped aside, broke the seal on the one you had been handed. You read it standing there, at the window, read it again, your knees in a sudden lock. "Move on," the others called at you, and you finally heard them. You put yourself back at the long tail end of the line, which had only gotten longer. Your eyes full of heat for all the Finleys, and especially for Peggy.

You slip Crumbs from your pocket, watch the mouse turn on the wheel of your palm as he hunts for a dusting of Schmidt's, which now you provide. Well done, Crumbs. You make a desperate wish toward running all the way to Philadelphia, miles back to South Twenty-third, you'd follow along beside the rail line, you'd kick off your boots when they're hurting, you'd carry Crumbs in your right pocket, flag a horseman with a cart at the big train station, and ride the rest of the way to Peggy.

It isn't right that you're here and not there. It isn't right to be gone for a war, dressed like a soldier, rounds of ammunition your language now, the kinds of gas that kill, the weights of horses that will carry the guns versus the weights that will carry the dead. You can't keep the machines of yarn straight in your head anymore. You can't believe in roving. Worsted or wool, what does it matter now. Pops Finley is dead, and you're nowhere there, and Harry put it in a letter because the girl you love is too flat shattered to lift her hand and tell you.

You have two letters in your pocket. What kind of cruel will you be? You need to tell, you can't, about the rumors you have heard, nothing official yet, nothing top-down confidential, but you've overheard talk when you've been down among horses, when nobody could see you in the shadows. You need your news to be known, or else. You need to be by her side when she hears from you, hold her so she doesn't fall. "She's fragile," Harry had written. "We've all gone flimsy."

The men with half their names are smoking through their wait in line, the longest wait you've ever seen. Everyone sticking a stamp on the gossip that has come down. Everyone has somebody they're hurting. You feel Crumbs turning a nest in your pocket. Let the murine sleep. You hear the buzz of a fly, swat at the skin of your neck.

You lean against a post and close your eyes and a day fugues back. It's Ma Finley planting a box of pansies by the stoop, and you and Peggy at her side, deciding on the arrangements of the yellows and the purples, the pansy faces looking like bonnets. Pops is near, on the stoop steps, pretending to read yesterday's paper, but you notice how his head is turned, and how he's watching Ma with a look you can't decipher.

You search your memory now, hold Pops's face as it is—round like the rounds of his spectacles, pale as the moon, his thin lips parted as if he'd like to have a word. You wonder if, sitting there, he was counting out his fortune, taking the whole of his abbreviating living in. A good long look at Ma, to rock him for eternity.

You hear the men agitating from behind. You step into the breach that, in front of you, has widened. All these men posting their letters home, kissing off postcards, some of them saluting to Crumbs, as they pass you on their way out, back to the Camp and its barracks and its trenches, the days that are running so short now. Crumbs's nose sniffing over your pocket.

The line hauls itself forward. The window is in view. You have two letters in your pocket, and you will post just one. Tomorrow, you think. Tomorrow or the next day, you'll post the second one. Either choice is cruel and you only have two choices, and none of this is what you'd choose.

Jennie

gets the news because she works the honey stand, and because Farm Fresh isn't far from Bee's Sweet at the Market. News like this travels quick as the brats down the sawdust corridors, loud as the trains overhead. The boy's brother is who came her way to tell her—a red-headed kid who looks nothing like Peggy's beau and nothing like his father, either.

"Ma'am," the brother says, being full of politeness. "Ma'am, we got a letter."

The crumple of the thing is dug out as proof. The boy's handwriting is neat and square. Jennie places her hand against her chest and presses hard to steady her heart's beating. She steadies herself against the stacked crates that hold the honey jars, in which the combs still float, little bits of the bees' business.

"Thank you," Jennie says. And (she remembers to say it, for this is a brother, too, and that, across the Market, is a Pa): "I am so sorry."

It will be up to her to convey the news, but she can't do that. She loves her sister in ways she never would confess; what would be the good of such confessing? It's easier to complain about the rumpus in the parlor (not anymore) or the prejudice in chores (though a fairness settled once the boy went off to Meade and Peggy was less high on distractions) or the disturbance Peggy would make at night, talking in her dreams (but Peggy sleeps with Ma now, and the sister bed is bigger, and there's more room for Jennie to cry out herself, calling her Pops home).

Peggy's been something for her smarts and Jennie's been something for her beauty, and what could the point ever possibly be, to burnish Peggy with outright affection? Between them, since Pops's passing, a balance has been struck, but now Jennie has news that Peggy will need, and she doesn't want to be the one who tells it. To lie outright, saying "It'll be all right" or "Don't you worry." Because there's plenty of reasons to worry.

Jennie sees the paper, too, the news of Sunday arriving on Wednesday, the numbers of the war dead growing higher.

A customer's wanting two jars of honey. Jennie takes the cash. A brat has an order for Jennie to fill. Jennie does the counting. All this time, she feels the eyes of the boy's brother on her, and, on occasion, the glance of the Pa. She's steady on her feet, for Uncle Sam has called for courage. She's a patriot keeping a tally of the cash as the jars disappear at the Market.

The words you make

with your breath and tongue are words not another soul can see. Jennie tells no one. Then Jennie tells Harry. Then Harry crosses the street, to Lani's house, and Lani says, "All right then, I will do it." Knowing where Peggy will be, for it's Wednesday, an hour past the end of the first work shift, a concert day. Lani, through her open bedroom window, a dragonfly buzzed into her room, had heard Peggy reminding Ma just that morning on the stoop. "Don't be worried, Ma. I'll be an hour late." Lani knitting a first-suit for the girl she'll call October.

"There'll be nobody with a name like hers," Lani had said, proud, when she told Peggy. "It'll be impossible to forget her birthday."

Lani is getting her color back. She's knitted four first-suits now, most of them doughboy colors, you can't say she's not busy. The Lani of a thousand causes, even if some of them contradict.

She knows the way to Fleisher's because she's walked it plenty. Hung on the fence as the Bloomers showed their stubborn Sunday prowess off. Stood by the entrance to chaperone Peggy in the days just after Pops's passing. Pearl on the one side and Scoops on the other as Peggy left the building. Then Lani taking the chaperone's place as Scoops and Pearl went off to practice.

"See you tomorrow," Scoops would say, throwing baseball signs in their direction.

"Let's get you home," Lani'd say. Lani going everywhere now with a fake gold wedding ring. Lani saying that if you look straight ahead and walk your speed you'll get to where you're going safer.

The baby inside her doubling up on her heroics.

There's more light now in the days and Lani's been feeling braver, but today she needs more courage. All the way to Twenty-sixth and Reed she rehearses what she might say in the order that she might say it. She'll ask about the concert first, that much is sure. She'll ask what Miss Theiler had to say about the music that was playing. Maybe get to the matter of Pearl's limerick practice, or Scoops's pinochle habit, or tell me again how the self-acting mule works; it's much more complicated than drowning coconut goo with liquid milk chocolate. She'll let some silence grow between them at any rate and soon.

She'll wait until they're three blocks from home, and then she'll tell Peggy, merciful with her tone. Peggy's eyes will swell, like the first rise of a bruise. Lani doesn't know what will come after.

What if nobody knows

what will come after? What if the very velocity of this story's becoming—in the earliest morning hours, the sun rising over my left shoulder; in the late afternoons, the speared russets softening in the oven; in the evenings, the Elvino V. Smith map of the 38th Ward, scale 300 feet to an inch, on my lap as I walk the streets with Peggy, move her south past Manton, Latona, Titan, Beard, move her north, past Alter, across Washington, hurry her from the fringes of the city toward the rising glamor of it, then through, to the gray weather of the Baldwin complex—what if all that has begun to discommode my imagination?

What if my mood, and so my pages, saturate with mourning for a girl and a world agitated into being by a box that arrived decades late, on a Thanksgiving day, when we were celebrating Christmas. The circuitous route and labyrinthine fate of a story.

I could stop it now, leave Peggy where she is, in late June 1918, a score of levitated music in the fog beneath her thoughts. Hannah eating a melting ice cream in the middle of the street, and Lani beside her, each day growing bigger. Lani's hand with the fake gold band pressed upon her own rounded belly as she walks, collecting the telegraph signals of her baby. Lani arranging the order of her telling, the interludes of silence, out of kindness for the girl who saved her twice—once on the evening of the violence itself, then in all the rest of the days, talking her free of pennyroyal.

I could just stop.

These are just "snippets" from a time before you knew her, the woman I called my aunt wrote at the end of her two pages titled "Among My Souvenirs." *Perhaps, Lore can continue with how Margaret was involved in her church, her children, and in creating a warm, comfortable home for her family. I loved her dearly and knew I always was welcome in her heart.*

Perhaps, Lore can continue. But Lore did not. My mother is buried into the infinite quiet of a hill beside my father, their memories marked by the same pink granite stone that marks the memory of my grandmother. The sky above them is the weather. The weather is a kind of remembering, the kind in which truth dissolves into the skin of the imagination. We say we could stop—stop remembering, stop imagining—but we cannot. The story becomes its own velocity, and we are without power. In the telling of every story there are consequences. We dare them. In the mesmeric negotiation between the truth and fiction, the page still turns, the silence trances. Lani has whispered into Peggy's ear. A fluff of stuff is coming loose from Peggy's hair and drifting off behind her, bobbling away in her city of yarn, in the year of doughboy khaki.

I have lost count of the days. I cannot be trusted to keep it straight—which tomorrow will bring which news, which day is finally Sunday, which yesterday won't stop it.

They will reach

Hoboken by troop train. All the boys of the 314th Infantry Regiment, of the 79th Division, of the American Expeditionary Forces. And the other boys, too. And the horses in the big boxcars in the 40 x 8 coming up behind them, and the flies buzzing at the rear. And not boys. *Men.*

Swapped out of the lives they had been living and dug into the trench mud of Meade. Paraded in April. Packed up for battle in July, get your war faces on. General Kuhn and his staff already on their way, sailing the U.S.S. *Calamares* toward battles they will never be prepared for, or only in imperfect ways. The U.S.S. *Leviathan* in the harbor, waiting.

This is how the Philadelphia War History Committee will tell it, in their history produced four years on, the year of their writing being 1922, when Scoops has left Fleisher's for Chicago Ball and Pearl is back in London, where her father's from.

On July 8, the Leviathan (formerly the Hamburg-American liner Vaterland) sailed from Hoboken with the Division Headquarters, Headquarters Troop, 310th Machine Gun Battalion, 157th Infantry Brigade complete (313th and 314th Infantry and 311th Machine Gun Battalion), and the 304th Field Signal Battalion—more than 12,000 men.

More than twelve thousand strong—men who will have ridden the rails north, toward the city from which they came, then past it. Not all the boys emanating from Philadelphia, of course. Some boys from anthracite hills. Some from Pittsburgh. Some still speaking the native languages of their homelands—Hungary, Greece, Lithuania, Sicily, which has always been separate from Italy. But the boy who matters to this story will board the train at Odenton with the tatter of his book in his bag, her letters in that book, his Crumbs in his pocket. Crumbs a full-grown mouse by now, the unofficial mascot of the 314th. Nobody, and especially not the boy, leaving Crumbs behind.

The *Leviathan*, formerly the *Vaterland*, is a prized Hamburg-American liner, a luxury double-bottomed, double-skinned beauty with a stacking of steel decks and a speed so fine it won't need escorts. It had been blockaded by the British and marooned in the Jersey port until the German U-boats changed the tide of things and the United States Shipping Board seized what wasn't theirs and shouldn't have been the Germans', either. The Americans made the ships their own—retrofitted best as time and materials allowed, then sent the 288-foot-wide and 166-foot-high liner sailing with new troop cargo across the frothing sea.

The boy rides the rail, south to north, past the tilled earth and red barns and baled hay that have supplied the industry of his training, the nourishment of the horses, such as that's been. Past the clamor at the minor depots. Past the townsfolk who are clustered out along the iron rails and softwood sleepers, some of them with well-wishing signs, some of them advertising the death that will soon slay the Kaiser, some of them tow-headed children just running along, barefoot and dusty with ballast, too close to the tonnage of the train, too dangerous.

Above the rivers and lakes on the trestles of bridges.

Through the near trees, emerald green now with summer. Emerald. Toward Hoboken, which is toward Philadelphia, which is coming now, it's coming.

The Philadelphia boys are standing. They are crowding up against each other, an active compress of uniforms and doffed caps, rifle-hardened shoulders and chafed hands, faces reengineered by the awkward configurations of gas masks. They are jostling for a chance to glance through the rectangular panes of the train, to look one last time on their inconceivable erstwhile lives, the place where they'd come from. The heaving smoke of their workshop city. The brown murk of their agitated river. The dry-docks and mud banks, the occasional reeds, the birds rising from the reeds while the train with its miles, seems like miles, of men and horses rattles on. The birds dropping their feathers.

And now vaudeville and City Hall and the spiked spires of churches in the distance. The glass and stone and brick of the places they remember as John Wanamaker or the Automat or the Walnut Street Theater—impossible to see from the rails but proclaimed by memory, hot as desire, specific as truth, and as need. It all coming back as the train trundles on, as everything they've left behind lies forward, but only in this moment.

With his hand protective over the mouse in his pocket, the boy jostles for his chance. Raises an elbow. Collapses a shoulder. Strains to see. Reed Street. Wharton Street. Gray's Ferry. Washington Avenue.

Taking a guess through the smudge and the smear, squinting across the great maw of the smoking distance. She is out there somewhere, the girl to whom he finally sent his letter. *I'll be home quick, Peggy, you'll see.* She is watching the bird feathers fall from the sky. She is keeping them safe in her pocket. Her face rearranged by the grief of Pops's dying, by the hours she spends now before the stamp of the self-acting mules at Fleisher's, before the piano player's concerts on Wednesday afternoons that hollow out the ache in her and then make the ache come harder.

They will have to hold the crowds back, as the troop train trundles. They will hear the people holler, watch them wave the paraphernalia of patriotism, the stars and stripes, the painted placards, their shirt sleeves and their blouses. It will be like a puzzle dropped to the floor, a scene in the scatter of so many confusing pieces, and he will feel the warm hunch of Crumbs in his pocket, the weight against his heart, now an elbow at his rib cage, another boy straining to see.

But who will be able to see, who can see? Who will know if the girl will be running there, standing there, beside her brother Harry, beside her Ma, a widow now, beside Lani, growing to be a mother? Who will know who is out there in the crowd, and where the crowds will be, and such an uproar it will be, such a wild, bewildering holler.

Toward Philadelphia. Past Philadelphia. Haste speed. The boys are needed in Europe because an assassin, on June 28, 1914, shot the Austrian

Archduke Franz Ferdinand and his wife, a dark-haired aristocrat with aristocratic posture named Sophie. Because Bosnia had been annexed into the hunger of the Archduke's empire. Because people were slaughtered in the aftermath. Because one country made war, and then another, until the war was in the seas, and then the war was in the States.

An assassin. A few bullets. And a war.

The sound among the men will drop to a low, deep nothing when there is no more Philadelphia through the panes of troop-train glass. Philadelphia will be behind them now, and the war will be even closer, ahead.

In Hoboken, there'll be a parade up a dozen blocks of First Street, and boys even younger than the boy offering to carry his knapsack, offering sandwiches on fresh bread. Straight-backed, the boys will stand, saluting. Yes, please, to the sandwich, a nice smear of mustard on it, better than the mustard at Meade. No to the carrying of his knapsack.

It's his whole life in there, it's everything that matters. He'll parade the dozen blocks imagining Peggy in the crowds—Peggy running all this way, a silver pail with a hot lunch in it, a letter for him, pages and pages. He'll imagine her fighting her way through the crowds, smashing into the force of the parade. Of stopping every last boot stomp so that she might kiss him, her body flung against his, her heat.

It was his face

through the troop-train pane. It was his, she's always known it, carried it with her through all the years, the years ending now, or shortly. His eyes, like the river after rain. No other eyes like his. His mouth, no other split like his between those two front teeth, at just that distance, just that tilt. His three-inch brim Montana Peak hat, felt-manufactured and grommeted, leather chin-strapped and clapped high on his chest with the hand she recognized. His hair maybe shorter than she'd ever seen, but the curls in it still making an unruly show of themselves.

Calling out his name, calling, maybe he might hear her. Might hear Harry, who had taken off behind her, his good suit on, running the streets fast as she did, running toward the rail lines, toward the river.

The whole eternity of the one brief moment trundling through her mind, now more vibration than scene. Her husband downstairs in the parlor watching the best channel on TV. How much time is left to her now? Two days? Three? She moves her hand across the bedspread and remembers the day she bought it at John Wanamaker, with the money she'd saved up from Fleisher's.

Money she had not spent until long after her wedding day. Until she'd settled in, at last, with the life she had. A beautiful white cotton arabesqued with fine white-thread leaves, a cloth you had to touch to see. Cotton, not wool, but she could see it. She'd stood alongside the Golden Eagle of the John Wanamaker store until she'd gathered the gumption to buy the spread, to take it home, by way of trolley, to the life she had now. A bedspread snapped free of its folds in the air above the bed, then dropping, slowly, slowly down.

Easing off the wrinkles with her hand.

A few more tokens—

Among my—

and is this what the song finally means? This white arabesqued bedspread, thin and worn, keeping her company now while she remembers
what she is certain she saw—the boy's face smudging by, the boy, looking
in the slight wrong tilt of direction, how could he ever see her?

The dusting of the gravel beneath the throttle of the train.

The smoke that became the measure of the distance.

Leviathan

The flavorful atmosphere of the harbor as your ship set off in its camouflage stripes toward the war. The tugboats so entirely minuscule in proportion to their purpose. The eyes of the thousands of men, out on the squeeze of the decks, turned west, looking back, and what was the mood? Your mood was melancholy. Your mood was the electric lights of your country blurring the scene in your head. The awesome silence now displaced by the words you did not yet understand—the exclamations of Italians, Austrian, Hungarian, Poles, Serbs, the men from the coal mines and the mountains, who had their own way of speaking, and somewhere in the multitudes were the members of your 314th, you just had to find them, for you'd wandered off, you were desperate for a last view of the harbor.

Your billet number and your instructions in your pocket:

Keep quiet.

Follow guide directly to your compartment.

Find your bunk by number.

Remain in your compartment until release sounds by bugle.

Locate latrines and urinals.

Read and digest booklet of orders and instructions issue.

Familiarize yourself with plans of ship.

You'd grown accustomed to the unfathomable. The width of the streets between the infinity rows of wooden barracks, regimental structures, water tanks, YMCAs, the machine shops and mangy horses of Camp Meade. The plentitudes of the roll-up beds hauled out into the air, so that they might be aired, on doughboy cleaning day. The heaving quantity of the bayonets hoisted up onto uniformed shoulders during the long hikes in the hot hills. Two miles. Five. The cardinal sins of the mess halls, the sizable stretch of the laundry house, the proportion of the laughter on vaudeville night at the Liberty Theatre. Whatever was funny was twice as funny. The circle of men thrown to the ground learning not to waste their bullets. The white peaked tents bulking up the in-between, over here, over there, make capacious room for the crowded new selectees. The end-to-end of the buck-the-Huns lines. The intervals of donkey carts bringing up the rear for the machine-gun companies, who had been out in the woodlands, training, and the forks in mess hall, and the quantities of boys who danced with other boys while the Victrola played, or who stripped down for a friendly boxing match, or who threw their jackets to the dust to play the full and lazy protractedness of baseball.

The number of the singers, singing.

It's a hard thing to lick the Kaiser, it's a hard thing to do,

It's a hard thing to lick the Kaiser and we know that is true.

Goodbye, Russian quitters, England, France, and Italy stuck true.

But there's one flag that will lick the Kaiser,

It's the Old Red, White and Blue.

Still. Nothing of that vastness was anything like the vastness of the *Leviathan*, a thousand feet long, a hundred feet wide, and so tall she couldn't fit beneath the Brooklyn Bridge as you pulled away from harbor, past Lady Liberty, wearing the shrouding of night. The *Leviathan's* decks were labeled A through H. Her connecting latches and hatches and ladders and stairs were unmappable in your mechanical mind. The upper deck, yes, that was clear: The upper deck was lobbies and loungers. But after that, and below: the coal bunkers and stoker rooms, the galleys and first aid, the baggage holds, the lines in which you were to stand for your two meals a day, your prunes and beans. The dimensions were as claustrophobic as the quarters themselves, which were eight men to a compartment, your beds built of iron pipe and mesh, your eyes staring up at the writhing of another man's thin mattress. And this was July. And the portholes were sealed. And the air was thick. And the seasick cans were filling. You were responsible for cleaning up your sick.

The smell of the sweat and the sick. No C.C. pills could cure it.

Instructions: Be stealth. Do not whistle. Do not hum in the dark. Do not drop a single letter overboard, or splash your hat or spectacles, for any trace you make is a flare, proof to the enemy that you're coming. The enemy cannot know that you are coming.

No striking of a match on deck at night. No smokes beneath the stars. No mirrors catching starlight. No going anywhere without your life preserver strapped upon yourself. No losing touch with your murine, keep Crumbs tight and safe in your seafaring pocket, keep Crumbs fed and satisfied. Stay close with the men of the 314th, with Private Ricci, in particular, who has a sweetheart back in Scranton, pictures of her that he keeps in his pocket, you could be her sister, Peggy. Or you could be her cousin.

Keep your eye on the many horizons, which go on endless and are haze and wave-lap, gray and bleak, except on the day you spot the spout of a whale, out in the weary distance. You thought it was the Huns at first, shared your view of the situation with Ricci, who was standing there beside you, conducting a middle of the day good smoke.

Drawing it in.

Breathing it out.

You confided in Ricci that your end was near, that you'd be having a nautical funeral. How you were already doing the math in your mind—how far down you would sink, which fish would watch you sinking, how the ocean would taste when it drowned in through your mouth, through your throat, through your lungs. Drowned in, yes, Ricci, that's how I mean to say it. You were saying how lonesome it would be, dying in the sea, even if Jones and his pictures were beside you.

Going down.

But the boys standing beside you in the blazing sun had other speculations. Jones, too, watching you, with that way he had of smiling with his eyes. In so many languages that you can't speak you hear them say *sea monster*, which is precisely what your Hun turned out to be—a magnificent steam-spouting monster. And the next day there was another whale, or maybe it was the very same one, a whale anointing itself as unofficial chaperone to the AEF, to the thousands of boys on the ship.

This is the story you will tell Peggy, the thing that you will put down in the letter you'll write while lying shirtless on your back on the third bunk up. Every day you start again: *Dear Peggy*. You write it as the *Leviathan* plows forward, your handwriting changing with each new start, the tight loops loosening, the rightward slant shifting upright, the marks of grammar becoming increasingly unnecessary, for time runs ever shorter, and Crumbs has gotten loose and you must find him, and now it is your turn, again, for the four-hour watch, so you put your pen down and hide your letter beneath your pillow. You find the ladder and the hatch and the ropes, you find your way. You make your way to the deck, where you now stand quelling the boy beside you who shouts "Sub! Sub! Sub!" with his Chicago accent, even though, this time, and maybe just for now, the *Leviathan* is safe. It's just the sun glancing off the metal of the ocean.

"Quiet now," you say to the boy. For you are older now than you were yesterday and you know a monster from a monster.

Dear Peggy, It's dark at night in the bunk on the ship.

Dear Peggy, I can't remember worsted.

Dear Peggy, Do you remember the way the lion sang, and the elephant, too, and the chimp?

Dear Peggy, The whales have a song they sing. Or the one whale. I can't tell from the spouting.

Dear Peggy, We are a sundown away from the end of the sea, and we have company. Camouflaged destroyers who will keep us safe in the Hun-infested waters. We have gunners but the destroyers have speed, and we're coming toward land now, toward the rocky rise of Brittany, we've come this far and the Kaiser cannot stop us. Through the channel, to Brest. We're coming. We're nearing the war, but it's so hard to see. Fog, Peggy. Wish I could see you.

Dear Peggy, Crumbs is growing anxious.

Dear Peggy, Read me a story.

They had heard the insistent thrum of the machines,

the rumors of need, and come north for the chance of better living. North because crops were failing in the south, and because their lives were at risk at the hands of lynch mobs and pure racists, and because wasn't Philadelphia the City of Brotherly Love, wouldn't it be kinder?

They settled in among the other immigrants who had built the city—the German Americans, the Irish Americans, and the Italian Americans—the surges of those who'd arrived from elsewhere with their own one or two sacks and their staggering dreams. There was room, or so it seemed, on the fringes—in the row-house fabric of domestic life running south from Spruce Street toward Washington. Often multiples of mothers and fathers with their multiples of little ones crowding a few rooms and lining up for the one toilet, hanging interior laundry to achieve cleanliness and the slimmest possible iota of a private thought or moment.

The washtub in the alleyway.

The bedding on the pavement.

The cook fires congesting rooms built like corridors.

But those who had earlier fought for their own place in the fresh harbor of Philadelphia fought, as people do, against them and theirs. There were incidents, and they were growing. Racial epithets and graffiti. The stoning of the residence of Mrs. T. Lyle at 2504 Pine Street. The setting to flames of two full wagon-loads of furniture when yet another new immigrating family threatened to take shelter on that very same block of Pine, in that very same time frame. *We will ash your life. You don't belong here.* Even the families of the men who had joined the Armed Forces to fight on behalf of the good of the nation were endangered. Rank hypocrisy taking up arms in the Quaker town.

Adella Bond, employed by the municipal courts as a probation officer, was diminutive and young and had "light brown skin," according to the reports and the few historians who remember to write of her now. She had enough wealth, such as wealth was, to buy the house at 2936 Ellsworth Street, which stood not far from the Arsenal. The real estate agent whom she'd trusted had not bothered to caution her about the current of tensions in that part of South Philly, the threats being made and sometimes being carried out, but it wasn't long before, walking down her brand-new street, she learned of them for herself.

This was July of the worst year there was. This became headlines. This was stones hurled at a respectable, hard-working woman who kept walking. Adella Bond did not ask to reverse the mortgage papers, because that's not how real estate works. Instead, on July 24, she watched her furniture roll up the street behind the movers. She opened her door, let the furniture in, made her house a home. That was a Wednesday. Two days later, a Friday, some hundred white men filled Mrs. Bond's block of Ellsworth, shouting many terrible things, including the news that some among them carried guns.

Then a man handed a woman the baby he'd been carrying. He hoisted something heavy and hard. He threw it. The crash of glass. The thud of an inert intruder. Ugly coming in with the hot July air.

Tell me what you'd do. A woman, alone. An armed crowd in the street. Smashed glass crashing on the parlor floor of your brand-new, two-day furnished home.

What Adella Bond did was hurry up the stairs to her second floor. She found her revolver and cocked it. She opened her window and aimed, she would say, up, into the air, her SOS sign for the police she hoped would come to help.

Somehow, still, a bullet pierced the leg of the rock thrower. How dare she aim at him? Had she? Was that her bullet? The ensuing anger was unconstrained, it was violence. Read the newspapers of the time, work your way into the headlines.

Lone Woman Holds a Mob of 500 White Brutes at Bay: Adella Bond Shoots into Mob Attempting Violence (*Philadelphia Tribune*). And yet: **Mrs. Bond Determined to Occupy Her House** (*The Philadelphia Inquirer*).

The record implicates and disturbs the imagination. And if the rock thrower and his brother were arrested, so was Mrs. Bond, this inciter of a riot, whose valuables were ransacked and whose furniture was splintered when she was taken into custody. What had it been—less than a week?—since she'd taken possession of the house on Ellsworth, which was not far from the Arsenal.

Not far from Peggy and the Finleys.

Not far from Lani, a surge of alarm in her heart.

Not far from Hannah, young, taking it all in, remembering it years later, these stories she would tell.

That Saturday a Black man was accused of thieving, and when, pursued by a clerk, he defended himself, he was subdued, which is to say assaulted, by a crowd. On Sunday, Jesse Butler, on his way home from a party, was chased by an insatiable mob. Lifting his gun while running for the safety he could not find, he fired. His bullet struck a white man on that chase named Hugh Lavery. Lavery died. More anger massed, more violence. The demands for what the mob called justice.

Those newly arrived from the south seeking a better life, more opportunity, found, in Philadelphia, harsh words, harassment, intimidation, aggravation, worse. Those who dared to run for their lives, or to try to save them, could find themselves pummeled or arrested, chased into a hospital, then assaulted even worse by the police.

Right there. In the hospital.

Those who were part of the mob, on the other hand, and thousands, the historians say, were, would return at some odd hour of the night and day with damage they would carry for the rest of their lives—bruises on their backs, teeth gone missing, the ghost of a knife in their thighs, boot stomp. And then there was the witness wives and children bore—watching the oxygenated terror behind the bars hammered across window panes.

2 Slain, 20 Injured As 5000 Fight Race War in South Philadelphia: Two Square Miles in Downtown District is Ground of One of Bloodiest Conflicts of Kind in History of City—Battles Rage Fiercely for Hours—Shock Causes Death of One Victim's Wife (*Philadelphia Inquirer*)

Police Captain William Mills shuts down the saloons; that doesn't help. The police officers from five separate districts swarm the area, but the conflagration rages. Blackjacks. Knives. Sharp-toothed bricks. Brandished razors. Bruised and bloody fists. The glass of the windows that have been smashed in too many homes to count.

The marines are deployed to help, the sailors, more bluebacks. But hatred has a mind of its own. Its hunger feeds itself.

From Twentieth to Thirtieth Streets. From Lombard to Dickinson. Which is to say Twenty-sixth and Reed, and also 1123 South Twenty-third, the nexus of this story. My grandmother was there, sixteen, the heat of the city upon her and her streets, but I cannot see her, in my mind's eye, cannot plot her elegant height and dark hair, those tufts of yarn in her hair, that damning letter in her pocket, those more feathers, so many feathers, what is she doing with those feathers?—cannot plot all of this into those awful days in late July when her city seethed, when she was an Irish American among Irish Americans, striving like all others, to forge a life in the Workshop of the World, the Quaker City.

If I were to write what I cannot, in my imagination, see, I would be writing fiction. This is not a book of fiction. This is a book of what I see, and what I see is Lani, her belly, her baby within. What I see is Lani out in the streets, her face streaked with what you might call tears but what I will say is determination. Lani among the bruised and the beaten—cutting rags from the hem of her skirt to tie off a wound, hauling a bucket of water to a chased family in need. I see Lani now, bringing a hurt girl home, saying what was once said to her, the words that made her strong, the words that saved her: *There, there. I have you now. I'm here.*

And now here's Hannah, there at Lani's side, bringing an ice cream to the broken girl with pretty braids, pink ribbons in her hair. Hannah running home and running straight back now, with a doll tucked under one arm and a single lucky stone chip in her hand. Now it is Hannah and Lani, the two of them taking their best care—*There, there. We have you now. We're here*—and now at last it's Peggy my mind's eye sees—Peggy running through the narrow of her house and down the narrow of her stoop and across the street and into Lani's house, where the healing must begin, where a story wants for healing.

Tomorrow's News.

It comes.

August,

and the headlines are a litany of the atrocious. Every inch of the news more days late than ever, sometimes weeks, and soiled by the lingering fingertips of near neighbors. The news buckles, groans. It is creased by the heavy heat that has fallen down upon the city like a curse, scorching the horses pulling wagons in the street, suffocating the birds in the gutters, staggering the men and women at work in the swelter of their workshops. The news is ground down out of itself before Peggy even sees it. Then she sees it.

July 15: The Second Battle of the Marne, 85,000 American troops fighting the Germans east and west of Reims.

July 18: The start of the Aisne-Marne offensive, 250,000 Americans in coordination with the French gaining some momentum.

August 8: The Allied forces massed at Amiens.

More sugar rations. More Baldwin locomotives. More ships being built in the shipyards. More widows. More children who will grow up wondering who their fathers might have been, or who they might have been, with a father. More people dying now from heat, right there in the factories, war casualties, Peggy thinks.

Every grief being its own one grief.

The collective afflictions clinging like the clog of August's humidity.

Sunday's news. Last Sunday's news. And here comes Lani from across the street, beads of sweat on her upper lip and her dark hair tumbling toward where her waist once was—cascades of hair left loose across her surprising, expansive belly. Ma has loosened the seams again on Lani's cotton shift—hand picked the old threads out, hand stitched the new ones in. Still, the fabric strains against the kicking of the baby's feet, which stomp as if The American Quartet were still playing on the silenced Victrola.

"That's some October," Peggy will say, if it's not a working day or an errands day or a game day at the ball field, or if Fleisher's, like others of the factories in town, has closed due to the stifling, murderous heat. Lani will take a seat in the largest chair and Ma will bring her lemonade, minus the sugar.

Ma's hair has gone from gray to white, a sudden transformation. She is pale despite the summer sun. She leaves the house decreasingly, so others come to visit. Scoops, more often now. Pearl, when she's hungry. Jennie's new beau, whom she met at the Market—a man unfit for battle thanks to the swoon in his spine, but kind, Jennie says. Color in Jennie's cheeks as she says it. Kind enough, she corrects herself, for the time being.

But mostly it's Lani, religiously, who visits Ma each day—rescuing Ma from the absence in the house. They will talk the weather that has come on strong—the animals Lani has seen dying in the sun, the auto truck-load of chickens that dropped dead in their Market crates just last week, the mercury in the thermometers hitting 103.5 degrees, and the water supply so tapped out by now that there's no relief at the hydrants for alley dwellers.

Lani speaks of all this waving a fan before her face, toward her armpits, until Peggy comes in from a long day of doffing, and sits, the fluff in her hair trembling loose and sifting free, the heat of the day pooling in the hollows behind her knees.

Lani has regained her gift for talk. She's loose with her opinions. Her sentences spool and unspool, like a Fleisher's rhythm. Back and forth, a sense and a sound. Lani does the talking. The clock ticks. The day moves on. Lani is revolution, and rebellion.

But also, in this moment, weather. The baby. Lani's mother, who, despite the heat, sits most of the day in her stiff black dress, watching the window as if her husband will finally make his way home from his long skate over the thin ice of the Schuylkill River. As if, someday soon, the man she married will take up his old post in the cramped parlor and commiserate with the widow about her daughter's condition. Which the widow is still not speaking of. As if Lani's circumstance is an affliction.

Ma will shake her head. Peggy will complain. Lani will blow some air up through her bangs, fan her face, hold the pause, then change the rhythm, speak of the girl she brought home that day, dark-skinned and lovely and gone now, back home. She'll sit forward in the sigh of the stuffed chair, and rest her hands across the surprising girth of her baby, and Peggy will remember those hours when Lani stammered down the street and then her lust for pennyroyal.

"Painted a new sign," Lani'll say. "For the suffragists." Her cause now, her camaraderie. Leaflet Lani, Peggy sometimes calls her. Soapbox Sweetie. Lani doesn't mind. Lani has a place now in a condition of purpose, in a circle of women to whom it doesn't much matter that Lani has a baby coming with no father in sight, a baby whose name, Lani is steadfast, will be October. Lani is a regular at the meetings now, an increasingly excellent listener.

She says.

Ma shakes her head, smiles half a smile.

"You, Lani?" Peggy says. "Listening?"

She talks to prove it. Repeats the litanies and parables, the slogans more clever than any man could ever write; they should hire Pearl to write some limericks, don't you think, she asks of Peggy. Don't you? She reports on the history of inequality and its protestors, a self-anointed educator. "Lucy Stone," she says, spangle eyed. "Sojourner Truth. Eunice Dana Brannan." Until she settles on the dilly biography of Miss Alice Paul, born just across the way, in Mount Laurel, New Jersey, and raised by a suffragist to be a suffragist, which is, as Lani defines it, an unmockable word that translates into a woman seeking citizenship-standing. A woman asking for a say in the governance of a country sending men—and women—off to die in the spirit and the defense of victory.

Democracy.

The power of the people.

Women are people.

"Amen," Peggy says, loosening her boots now, letting her foot blisters breathe. She combs her fingers through her hair. The yarn dust rises.

Lani will grow twisted up with the irony of it—the women welders, doffers, operators, machiners, ammunition tenders—"You, Peggy, and Scoops and Pearl"—who have traded aprons and silk collars for overalls and boots to do the jobs that supply the machinery of war but cannot, in federal fashion, vote like men.

Lani's stuck, too, on the word suffragist, the soft and the hard of the consonants, a word that sounds like what it means. She could say suffragist all day long. She could boast on Alice Paul and her litany of degrees—biology, sociology, economics, law—from Swarthmore College, the New York School of Philanthropy, the University of Pennsylvania, and American University, not to mention the school of militancy, attended on the streets of London where the British activists trained her up in the arts of picket lining, window smashing, hunger striking, purposeful civil disobedience, while, during school hours, she studied social work.

"Education," Ma says. Giving Peggy that look that she does.

What Alice has achieved, in Lani's estimation, is pure, plain history, no less prodigious than a general's battle strategy. That march up Pennsylvania Avenue in 1913 on the eve of Woodrow Wilson's first inauguration—sash and skirt, brigade and floats, Inez Milholland on the back of a white horse, and Wilson wondering where his own crowds had gone.

That "Grand Picket" of March 4, 1917—the one thousand women in the hard knock of frigid rain. Those silent sentinels who take their pickets to the White House lawn—"President Wilson: How Long Do You Advise Us to Wait?" "Wilson Is Against Women"—and stay, months going by and the women still standing there, holding their ground through weather and worse, the anti-picketers and police.

Boys attacking the women on the lawn. Men yanking the placards from their grips, smashing them to bits, roughing them up while they stand there. The police conducting arrests and the women tossed into the Occoquan Workhouse, where there are worms in their soup, chains on their wrists, torture and ridicule. The incarceration of Alice Paul herself, the educated Quaker who is soon transferred to a psychiatric wing, and isolated, in a jailhouse in DC, and who is eating nothing, shutting her mouth to the men who think they can force the mush down her throat. They cannot force her to live. She'll die if she has to. From her isolation cell, Alice gets a letter smuggled out—news of the violence of this incarceration, against her and against the others.

No one was supposed to know, but Alice will not be silenced. She and her women are women, which is to say, Lani says, indefatigable.

Every telling of the story is as emphatic as the last, and Ma and Peggy listen, captives in their own house to Lani's social call, her unyielding bedazzlement. Alice Paul, the woman who will not be defeated. Alice Paul, who endures what men might say and men might do, who turns injustice into action, starving herself into the news until Woodrow Wilson, a stalwart conservative with insatiable political ambitions, measures the shifting mood of the American people and decides that it's time to set Alice and the women free, and to endorse, at last, the Nineteenth Amendment in the worst year there'll be.

Lani leans over the wide girth of her child and slaps her own knee.

"What about that?" she says. "Ever seen anything like it?"

The vindication of Alice Paul is the hope that Lani's needed.

Alice Paul wins Wilson. But she isn't nearly finished. She needs the House to vote Aye, the Senate to agree, enough states to ratify the amendment that will give women, who are the better sex, the right to confirm or condemn with a ballot. Alice needs help, and Lani is there to help, Lani has her cause, her face red with the heat of her argument and the day.

Peggy offering Lani a second glass, fetching the pitcher from the kitchen, taking the smells of machine grease and lanolin with her, trailing tufts of roving, then coming back. Ma and Peggy watching Lani gulp it down, then sharing a glance between them. A few minutes of silence then, while Lani catches her breath.

"The sacred right to the elective franchise," Lani begins again. An old slogan but a good one. "Whose Democracy Are You Fighting For?" These are the words that Lani paints on the signs she makes and delivers to the cause. Each of her signs bolder than the last and made more intricate by an evolving final flourish of Lani's own design. She's become a regular artisan sign painter. She carries her proud work to the suffragists, a comical vision—she says so herself—the way she has to hold the sign way out in front of the baby who seems to dance all day long in her belly.

"I'm doing it for October," Lani tells Ma and Peggy. When she's done talking she drinks the lemonade down, her eyebrows knitting together beneath the beads of forehead sweat, for the drink missing its sugar packs a sour punch.

"Lani," Ma will say, after Lani stands and takes her baby with her, "has become a regular politician."

Ma will say it with a half-smile and a compressed face. She will say it looking past Peggy's shoulder, toward the bar of late afternoon sun striping itself down through the front door that leads to the stoop, left open at this hour on these hottest days, to rejuvenate the house with air.

Ma searches the atmosphere for Harry, who is maybe working late again, though the likelier story, on days like these, is that he's stopped at a saloon on his way home. That he's taken a stool amidst the smoke of the men who have not gone off to war, the men who are running the machines on safety's side, talking themselves into being their own kind of hero. There are fewer and fewer men in Philadelphia, and worst among the missing is Pops, and if Harry is needed at Baldwin's for a second shift, he's needed more at home, where he finds it harder and harder to be, in the company of Ma and the brokenhearted, during one of the hottest summers ever on record.

Because Harry can't fix what has happened to the Finleys. He cannot, with all his height and charm, his fine one suit and still fashionable hat, quiet the industrial noise in his city or salvage the news, which he reads after Peggy's finished reading. The news that has been handed down, from stoop to stoop, until it's his news that comes in later and later, older and older, but a fresh force of devastation every time.

FRENCH CROSS VESLE AND REACH AISNE RIVER WITH HUNS RETREATING FROM WHOLE MARNE SALIENT; SLIGHT MILITARY INTERVENTION IN RUSSIA U.S. PLAN (Sunday Morning, August 4, 1918, *Philadelphia Inquirer*)

AMERICAN LOSSES NOW OVER 12,000; 217 ON TODAY'S LIST | General March Denies Statement Latest Casualties Are 12,000 | Accurate Information Hard to Get—Exact Number Unknown (Sunday Morning, August 4, 1918, *Philadelphia Inquirer)*

963 U.S. Soldiers Pay Victory's Toll on French Fields | 86 Pennsylvanians, 21 Philadelphians on the Roll | Lieutenant Quentin Roosevelt Officially Reported Dead and Buried | Killed in Action | Severely Wounded in Action | Missing in Action (August 8, 1918, *Philadelphia Inquirer)*

He'll have a Gibson, please, Harry will. He'll have a Dark 'n' Stormy. Just one more sip before he heads home, but before he goes, he'll have another one, and after that a game of pool. The habit shames him, and he can't stop. He's breaking all the Finley hearts, and he cannot help it.

Ma holds her glance over Peggy's shoulder. She fixes the white in her hair. When the sun nicks the parlor just so, Ma sees how the yarn that has escaped her daughter's humid hair keeps floating. Fluffs and tufts of doughboy khaki cling to the middle air. They do not rise or fall.

"Now it's your turn," Ma will say to Peggy. "Tell me a story." And Peggy will start as she always does, if she's been to work that day, if the temperature has allowed it, which on this day, the temperature has, though it's still stifling. Peggy will deliver Pearl's best last limerick line of the day, which Peggy, during the lunch hour, will have strung up in her memory. "A real doozy this time, Ma," Peggy will say. "A holler and hoot." She'll replay the last line and then replay what Scoops said, for Scoops has become an excellent limerick critic.

If Harry still hasn't come home after this story's been told, Peggy will keep on talking. She'll say she thinks Miss Anne Theiler might be in love with the piano man who plays on Wednesday evenings because she polishes her boots for the recitals. She'll say that Scoops and her brothers are pitching long games of ball in the alley nearest their house, when the sun sizzles down and there is moonlight, "Has Scoops told you already?" She'll say that she may be getting a promotion one day, because Miss Theiler is needing a supervising assistant. And if Harry is still not home, she'll let the silence go by, and then talk about the boy she's missing. How she worries for him. How there's only been one letter. How impossible it seems that there is still a murine, living in a military pocket.

"Maybe it's just a bit of fiction," she'll say. "Like me, reading Kipling to Lani."

And after that, if they keep talking, and they will, the talk will turn to Pops. "Your turn," Peggy will say, "to tell a story," and Ma, so mostly silent all these hours long, will touch her hair and clear her throat and tell the story of meeting the only man she loved, the only man she can imagine loving.

"I found Pops outside the tailor shop down on Catherine Street," she'll say. "He was putting a good suds on the window."

"I can see it," Peggy will say, imagining. Peggy will always be a first-rate imaginer.

"It was like he was dancing with his hands," Ma will say. "I never saw a pair of hands like his. All through my living, Peggy. Never. I just stood there, watching, from across the street, and then I called out hello, and so he saw me."

"Never took his eyes off you since," Peggy will say. "Not unless he had to."

"The start of us," Ma will call the story, then sit in the stuffing of her own chair in the absence of Lani talking and remember what she won't have words to say.

It's Ma's best story. The start and not the end. Nobody likes the end of a story.

In the top left drawer of the dark dresser on the right side of the room, beneath

the silver mirror and the brush woven through with the strands of her hair, there is that velvet box, the color of a plum. Inside the box there are two smaller blonde-wood boxes, each box a cubic square. Into the lid of each box has been carved a gentle half-moon. Fit the tip of your finger-nail into the groove, and the lid will fall back on its copper-colored hinge.

The cubic square nested into the right side of the plum-colored box contains the pearl. A droplet of white at the end of a chain. This is what Peg wishes to give the girl, if only the girl would come back and sit in this room, beside her. Open the window. Reconvene the weather. Let the air breeze in, and the sounds that have kept watch over the time that, still, is passing.

The slight weight of the girl on the edge of the bed. The freckles on her face like the dot-to-dots she loved, the paperback activity book pressed open to a middle page, thin gray pages on the vinyl plane of the kitchen table. The girl holds the stub of a pencil in one hand. Her warm breath is sweet with the hint of canned peaches. The one single line connecting each dot to each dot has begun to indicate something discernable, a li-oness, it seems. Now a desert rock. Now a tree. A picture the girl hadn't seen before, until her pencil got working. The girl outlines the entire scene, then opens up her crayon box. The colors are arranged in the order of their heights, from the shortest crayon stub to the tallest. The black crayon is the tallest one, for the girl does not believe that black is a color. She does not believe in black at all. The tip of the black crayon is brand new, shiny.

The smell of crayon wax. Peg remembers.

If the girl would come back, Peg would lift the bones of her hand and gesture toward the drawer where the plum box lives. *Open the drawer,* she'd say. She would tell the girl to scoot her own hand around among the silk and cotton things—the lace slips, the nylon stockings, the Sunday underwear Peg has not worn for years; she'd refused to dress the cancer. *Go on,* she'd tell the girl. *It is the color of a plum, and it's soft as velvet, it's right there, have you found it?* and because the soft box would be just where Peg had left it, years now since she'd touched it, the girl would have no trouble at all gathering it up with her hand. *Found it,* she'd say, returning to the right side of the bed with the box in hand.

Choose the second box, Peg would say, as the girl lifted the lid on the plum velvet. *That one,* she'd gesture, her voice so soft she'd hope the girl could hear it. The girl wouldn't have to be told what to do with her nail; she'd choose the right box and pop the blonde-wood lid right open.

She'd lift the chain.

She'd loop the chain over her pointer finger and let the small white globe dangle. Hypnotic.

I had a friend, Peg would say, as the girl examined the pearl, moving her hand to catch a streamer of sun. *Her name was Pearl. This pearl was Pearl's pearl. She bought it with her money.*

With her allowance? the girl might ask, for the girl had heard the word from the kids on the school bus and from her friend Kelly, down the street, though she herself got no allowance. She had a pink pig ceramic bank with a painted corkscrew tail, but she didn't have an allowance.

With money she'd earned, Peg would say. *With the best last line of a limerick. She'd practiced,* Peg would say. *She'd earned it.*

It would be hard to know what the girl could understand about what a limerick is and why a last line matters; perhaps the girl's brother has already taught her limerick magic; he's a good boy, a smart one. *Pearl was the last-line winner, a big prize-winner,* Peg would say, carrying the story forward nonetheless, worrying less and less about what was making sense, for sometimes a story is only a rhythm and a rhythm is what makes a story and time was not on her side. *She'd put most of it away for her own education. But this pearl, well, this pearl, it was Pearl's memento. "My Philadelphia pearl," she called it.*

Peg would not go on about what had happened next. The truth would frighten the girl, who was only a child, dangling a bauble in the afternoon sun. Peg never had told anyone that next part of the story; like most of the rest of the life she had lived, she had kept it to herself. How Pearl had died a calamitous death. How, in dying, she'd left the pearl to Scoops. How Scoops had worn the pearl tucked into her baseball jersey until baseball took her half the way across the land to Chicago, where she would be the star of the team so that she could travel even more, up and down the east coast as a first-base legend. *It's a Philadelphia pearl,* Scoops had said to Peggy. *Pearl would want the pearl to stay in the city she loved best. With you. She loved you, Peggy.*

And so the pearl became Peggy's and she wore it just on Sundays, and just on other fine days, too.

Like the day her daughter got married to the man whose face was just like the girl's.

Like the days she went to Wildwood Crest, then drove along in her husband's Ford to the boardwalk at night, her best dress (*she was a fine dresser*) for promenading.

Like the first day at the gift shop on Fifty-second Street in West Philadelphia, when the early customers walked in and gave the whole arrangement of the thing a nod—the crescendo of gifts and candies, the crisp snap of the register, the bank rolls of new pennies and dimes, that sweet metallic smell.

Like the days she danced with her tall and handsome son, just like Ma and Harry had once done, before the worst year got even worse than it was, before what happened happened.

Pull her best dress on. Roll up the rugs. Put the needle down. Dance. Just to be upright again. The Charleston or Sinatra, she wouldn't care.

Among My—there it is again, her song.

It's yours, she would say to the girl, coming back to the end of the moment. *It's yours. Pearl's pearl. You're the one for it, Betty*

—

Boop—

Not imagining all the years from then when the girl, long since a woman, now a mother in a park with her son on a day made heavy by gray winter air, will touch that place just beneath her suprasternal notch, where the pearl has always hung, and recognize its absence. The pearl gone. The sheen. The tactile evidence of—

Everything lost in the moment, and what broke? The chain or the clasp?

There will be a parade,

but before the bugles and the steeds, the two hundred thousands of Philadelphians shoulder to shoulder, breath to breath across twenty-three blocks of the city, there will be early September when the murderer among them is lurking. Rumors, mostly, and from overseas, or from hospital wards, or from somewhere not far from Center City.

It's one of those days, when the weather is relief. Ma has come out to the stoop to watch a game of hopscotch being drawn out with some chalk. There they come, the rectangular boxes of the game laid out on the walk, She's careful, Hannah. She's neat, her black hair newly shortened by her mother's sewing shears and her skin so pale it seems she has escaped the blaze of summer sun and a new pink ribbon wrapped pretty around her wrist, a borrowed ribbon or a given one—I do not have that answer.

The other children on the block call out to Hannah. They watch from their second-story window perches overhead, directing the coalition of lines, the arrangement of numbers, insulting her drawn-out number five for looking precisely like her three, but Hannah doesn't care. She minds her own business. It is her hour in the setting sun. Her air on a day when the weather is relief. Her childhood becoming something else. This year she, too, will endlessly remember.

Now from her pocket Hannah slips a right-sized chip of stone.

All the flags of the children in their windows are gone. All that leaning out over the street. The sound now of doors opening and slamming shut, a cabal of children at the map of stacked rectangles.

"Gimme the stone," they say to Hannah. "My turn. Gimme."

She tosses the stone. She takes her first nice hop.

"Gimme," the kids say. She carries on. It's her chalk, her hopscotch, her stone.

It had rained in the afternoon. The street steams. Sometimes when Hannah tosses the chip of the stone it gets lost in the momentary fog. On the street she will stand, balancing on one naked foot, waiting for the steam to lift. The neighbor boys and girls will stomp their feet, impatient—"Get on with it now. Gimme my turn." But Hannah won't be budged. It's her chalk, her hopscotch, her stone.

Her self.

Peggy sits on the stone step beneath Ma, her thin red dress fanned out. It's Jennie's old dress with the hem remade for Peggy and two new pockets at the waist sewn on from fabric that Ma found in her old trunk. Peggy has been wearing this dress all through the swelter—this red dress, another gray dress, each of them improved by pockets. The pockets are where Peggy keeps her feathers, dozens of them now, so many birds losing their feathers. She has left her Little Libraries at home most of the long summer. There on the bedside stand, her side of the bed, where Pops once slept. Ma wakes less at night now, but she cries out in her sleep, and when she does, Peggy is there. "It's all right now, Ma." But it's not.

Pops's spectacles are still polished clean each morning. At night, when the full moon is up on the right side of the house, Peggy watches as they gleam. Peggy watches the kids, so much younger than she is.

"Joey first," Hannah says, down the street, relenting. "Joey, then Anna." It's still her game. She is in charge.

Lani opens the door to her own house and heads directly toward the Finleys, her big belly arriving before she does. There is no more room in the seams of her shift, nothing else Ma can do to make the old dress fit, so that the hem of it pulls upward past Lani's knees, which are Lani's only bony parts at this point in her condition. Even her hands have grown fleshy with the anticipation of birth, so that she ties a ribbon around her wedding finger now—the ribbon replacing the fake gold band—as if that would fool a stranger.

Before she even arrives, she is talking her famous blue streak. The new news of the suffragists. Her fervent belief in the signs she paints on behalf of female democracy. She's a woman of many causes, taken to cheering the suffragists, taken, too, to calling out the seditionists the second-hand news makes famous—the men and women suspected or accused of violating American trust by the austere members of the American Protective League.

She's keeping herself safe from the badge-wearing volunteers, the yellow-dog hunters, the anti-slackers, the vigilantes in charge of sniffing out the draft dodgers and pro-Germans, at pointing their fingers toward the whoevers who have willfully conveyed false reports and promoted the enemy's success. She is declaring herself all in for democracy and all for democratic women. Her fervor is her cloak of armor and her last defense. She has never since spoken of the late and awful afternoon when two men dragged her down an alleyway. She has a new last name for the strangers who ask, has taken to the kitchen with a borrowed copy of *Win the War in the Kitchen*. On this very day, in fact, she has come boasting of her apricot and prune marmalade, which tastes just right on the cornbread she's made to save on the wheat the doughboys must have for the bakeries set up across the front.

Lani is practicing being a mother now, building her safe harbor. She talks her blue streak. Ma lifts one eyebrow, plants one elbow on her thigh and catches her chin with her fist. Peggy only half listens. She has her eye instead on the hopscotch game, on Hannah directing traffic with her stone chip. She's a girl, Peggy thinks, growing up in a war, in a devastating year, with another child's ribbon at her wrist.

Hard to hear Lani over the residual sound of the mechanical mules in her ear. Hard to shake the throttle of the machinery of Fleisher's, the shake and the shudder in her bones now, the smells of the chemical dyes. She retreats into her private sphere, letting Ma laugh at whatever Ma is laughing at, and thinking of the letter, among the feathers, in her pocket. The words that have come at last, all the way from Brest. As if the boy is still on the watery seas but he's in the mud now, among the char of trees, on the road to where he's headed; it's all there, in yesterday's news.

We don't know where we are, he'd written, from the *Leviathan*. His k and his n and his w sliding into the circle among them.

The street steams. Hannah hops again. A dark-haired kid pulls out a whistle. Peggy imagines a whale rising to the surface, spouting. She imagines the foamed caps of sea waves crinkling out in all directions. She imagines the boy on the biggest boat there is, its portholes blackened, the lights gone out, the stars in an arc he cannot see from the spit of a bunk in a compartment of eight, hardly any room to breathe, he says, and Ricci the best friend he has, though a fellow named Horvath has taught him to whittle, and there's a Greek who sings so soft no officer in charge could hear him, and he likes that too, and have you played the bugle, Peggy? Are you practicing? Not much to it, all you do is move your lips. Embouchure.

She has not been practicing. The bugle's in Ma's trunk, with the lace and with the memories and with the two shirts and trousers that wait for Pops. But he's not coming home. The bugle waits for the boy to come home, or the bugle is for never.

The spout of the whale. Steam rising. Though the *Leviathan* has long since turned around, left the company of swift destroyers, and headed back in zigzag fashion to Hoboken, so that it might ship more men to war. Reinforcement men. Replacements.

The dark-haired boy blows out another whistle, but the girls have begun to clap Hannah on. Hannah, indefatigable in the late afternoon, the sky turning pink above the bare traces of steam. From further down Twenty-third, a strange sight comes ambling. A man like a beast, it seems, a human unhealthily proportioned—too wide at the torso, lopsided. Peggy lifts her hand to visor her eyes. She stands up from her stair on the stoop. Lani, suddenly silenced, turns in that direction, too, and Ma, and even Hannah stops hopping as the thing makes its way. It has a hat on, Harry's hat. It has Harry's shoes. It sounds like Harry, except that Harry's laughing. Peggy hasn't heard that sound since Pops's heart gave out at the Arsenal.

"What's this?" Lani says, the first to break the spell, when Harry's close enough and nobody need be asking questions. Because it's plain as the falling day what Harry's been hoisting with him, all the way from Baldwin's, Peggy thinks. All that long, long way.

"October needs a place to sleep," Harry says. "Doesn't she now?"

He lowers the cradle to the street—a long, wide, pine beauty. He barely brushes at it with the back of his hand and it rocks this way, that way, smooth and gentle. The headboard is taller than the footboard and cantilevers like a hood. The joints are pegged, professionally so. The sides are delicate with carving.

"My flourish," Lani says, when she realizes what Harry's done. Built her a cradle. Decorated it like one of her signs.

"October," she says, her voice dropped down into a whisper. "Will you look at what Uncle Harry has done. Like a princess you will be, in your cradle." She presses both hands against the bulging of her baby. She lets her tears run free, streaking the smudge off her end-of-day cheeks. Hannah and the hopscotch kids have lost every care they'd had for their game, the chip of stone now safe in Hannah's pocket, the kids in a throng around the three-stepped stoop where Ma is sitting still, Harry beside her now, his arm across her shoulder.

Peggy steps through the crowd, away from the circle, and looks back to see it all from a short distance, to frame it in her head, this shock of something beautiful inside the worst year there will be. Lani's face and broad chest, the start of the bulge of the baby tower above the shoulders of the kids. Lani's dark hair streams. Twilight is coming on. Hannah kneels now and the other kids too, to rock the cradle gently. As if October is already there, in their midst.

"What have you done?" Ma is asking Harry, her words quiet and grateful as if the thing he made with the scraps of the Baldwin yard and the help of a few good men, the thing he carried all that way, miles across town, was a gift for her. It is. There's no stink of whiskey on his breath. No slouch in his posture. No unsteadiness in the arm across her back.

His eyes are clear.

"Baby needs a place for dreaming," Harry says, speaking for them all. Yes, Peggy thinks. A place for dreaming. She crosses back and through the circle of admirers, fits her hands inside her pockets and kneels. One by one she lays her feathers down. A softness forms on the surface of the wood for the baby who is coming soon, who will sleep, when the right time comes, in a cradle Harry's made in the Workshop of the World, and with time that Peggy had lost track of.

Was it the chain or the clasp that broke?

Was it the creek or the mud that swallowed it whole?

Was it a lie that I never told my mother what I'd done?

I lost the pearl. I lost the pearl. I lost the pearl.

When I went the next day and the next day and afterwards, there was no sign of what I'd worn around my neck. As if a bird had stolen the pearl for her nest.

A book that is not a novel that is not a memoir can never be amends.

At first it seems so far away.

Just a rumor, as they say.

In April, at Fort Riley, in Haskell, Kansas: More than five hundred hospitalized, three dead. Throughout the summer, in army encampments west and south: sporadic outbreaks, deadly sequels. Malaise and crisis aboard naval ships. New words from the theater of war: Purple death. Flanders fever. Purulent bronchitis. Spanish flu.

Just a sore throat, just some chills, a fever. Then the drowning of the lungs.

There was already enough squeeze in the headlines in that year that was. Already too many rumors that nobody could prove taking inches in the papers that were thumped from door to stoop down South Twenty-third. Maybe it was a military disease. Maybe it would stop. Who says it will not stop: You couldn't expect things to get worse than they already were. At least Peggy couldn't. Have some fortitude. Wouldn't. Not now. Not, especially at night, the moon fighting its way in and Ma lying at her side, fitful in her sleep, calling for Pops with half-words, no commas. And Jennie coming home later than she should. And Harry working two harder shifts now. He was thinner. He was older. He was pale.

The others wherever the others were. Peg, remembering Peggy, can't keep track.

Peggy has had a visit with Mrs. Martine, Miss Theiler at her side. A good long talk in the office on the highest floor of Fleisher's, the art on the walls promenading up to that room having been lately rearranged, the rumor was, by Mr. Samuel Fleisher himself. He knew the artists by their names, the people said. He sometimes stood behind them as they drew, encouraging the vigor in charcoal lines, the expressive thickness of the paint.

Peggy had stood in the hall, alongside Miss Theiler, not talking, just waiting for the appointed time with Mrs. Martine. She'd been called to it. Interrupted. No one had explained. And then she'd stood in that hall studying the pictures inside their frames, missing—it was September now—the smell of chalkboard chalk, the symmetry of desks and chairs in classrooms, the talk about nothing with girls silly on love. The quiet in a room after a quiz has been given out. The having the answers to questions. Mrs. Rains.

Mrs. Martine wore a ripple-stitched suit with a pineapple-stitched trim. Her hair had been set. She had lip paint on. Her lashes curled back from their half-moon lids. Mrs. Martine was not disturbed by the underlying racket of machines. She was beautiful, Peggy thought, sitting there in her chair before the desk of Mrs. Martine. She was spectacularly pristine.

"Miss Theiler tells me that you are among the Fleisher best," she'd said. "That she could use your help as supervising assistant."

Miss Theiler had dressed for the occasion, too—straightened the knot in her hair, buffed her boots. She'd placed her hand over Peggy's when Mrs. Martine said her words, a shock of intimacy, Peg thinks now, re-membering then, when she was Peggy and young, suddenly prominent in a private meeting on the best floor of the best factory in the Workshop of the World, the home of doughboy khaki.

The smell of the wool dye rising up through the floors was heat. The smell was color, and Peggy's senses slid past and confused themselves, a condition she'll pass on to her granddaughter.

Imagine a granddaughter.

There'll be more bones, with supervising. More to give to the men who come to collect what is owed, then some. More to tuck into the darned toe of a sock so that when the sock grows fat she will slim it back, stuff some in her pocket, and ride the trolley to Wanamaker's, to buy Harry an Eckert with a silk red band, and Jennie a tangerine-colored col-lar, and Lani's baby a wooden rattle boisterous enough to accompany Lani's songs.

Or,

if the weather's not worse and her boot blisters have healed, she'll walk east and north to the city's finest market—the dark rumble of trains overhead, the hustle of farm vendors, the hollers of the brats more brazen for coin. She'll stand where she stood when she'd first looked up and the boy had found her. She'll buy Ma a fresh pint of raspberries then, a burlap of Brussel sprouts, some rutabaga. She'll say hello to the boy's father and hello to his brother, and ask them, quiet, counting out her change, "What have you heard? Have you had letters?"

The office's gone silent. Peggy looks up. She finds Mrs. Vera Martine's eyes steady upon her. There are some rules Peggy's to heed, does Peggy understand? She does, or she'll ask Miss Theiler later. There's women, longer at Fleisher's and older, too, who will have their envy toward Peggy; kindness is the solve for envy. There'll be a different apron to wear, and some reporting to do, and Miss Theiler says Peggy is good at calculating and Peggy nods and remembers to say thank you.

When Miss Theiler stands, Peggy stands.

When Miss Theiler opens the office door, Peggy steps through, ahead.

When Miss Theiler hurries down the hall, Peggy stops before the paintings on the wall, one particular painting, the thick accumulations of color that approximate the Schuylkill. The artist has scrubbed off the muck and filth. No smokestacks. No abattoir. No coal docks. The artist has set the river running clean, dabbed birds and bridges overhead, slashed a nick of sun on one rock along the banks, brushed two people in their leisure, walking.

"We'll miss lunch," Miss Theiler says. "If we don't hurry."

She finds the bugle

between a wrinkle of lace and the threads of a hooked rug in Ma's trunk, beneath Ma's bed. She finds it there because she'd buried it there on the day he left for Meade. In the half-dark of the late part of that February day, she'd knelt beside the bed, drawn the trunk across the floor, cleaned the latch of a single spider web with her skirt hem, and put the thing to sleep.

She'd been the last to leave the platform at the B & O, at 24th and Chestnut, she and Harry. The crowd was gone but she'd remained. The train was vanished, but she'd waited, as if the war might reverse itself and the train might return. As if the dust of the ballast would rise and smoke but not ghost, and there'd be so much commotion and so much gorgeous shake-up through the soles of her worn high-tops through the sudden empty hollows of her bones. Until Harry finally said, "Come on, now, Peggy. Let's go home."

She finds the bugle, which is a brass G bugle. She finds its second-hand mouthpiece, built, the boy had said, for a trumpet. It's Sunday afternoon and Ma is asleep on the parlor chair downstairs, a ball of doughboy yarn at her feet, the dropped stitches of a pair of doughboy socks on her lap. The other rooms in the cramped house are awful with absence. Where Jennie is, where Harry is, she does not know. Lani's at a meeting. She left this morning wearing her too-tight dress, Liberty Loan buttons punched into her collar.

Peggy had watched her go, through the windowpanes of Ma's room in the house on South Twenty-third.

She writes a note for Ma and leaves it on the kitchen table. *Don't worry.* She doesn't pull her boots on until she's outside on the stoop, the door closing like a whisper behind her. There's a letter, his last letter, in one of her plain-gray pockets and the Kipling Little Library in the other. She walks halfway north, then knocks on Hannah's door and the dark-haired girl answers like she's the only person home. "It's a good book," Peggy says, giving the Kipling now to Hannah. Says nothing more than that.

"You play the bugle?" Hannah asks, the green faux leather in the palm of her hand. Her dark eyes wide with the surprise of her Sunday caller.

Peggy walks backwards down the two steps, then turns to keep on walking, calls back over her shoulder.

"Learning," Peggy answers. As if it could all be as simple as that.

It's a long way to her rock by the river. She has time. It has started to rain, a soft interlude that falls like feathers. She keeps the bugle dry by slipping it up toward her flat belly, beneath the cotton of her shift, an awkward maneuver she performs in an alley when she's sure no one is looking. By the time she arrives at the stretch of lawn beyond the boat houses, her hair is wet and the Sunday strollers have taken refuge inside and there are hardly any scullers still out there on the horizon, and she does not mind.

She is glad for the companion of the river, for the thought of the animals on the west bank, in the zoo, for the memory of him on the spotted mule in the snow, for the letter in her pocket, which she has shielded from the rain with the flesh of her hand, across all these blocks of the city.

The rain ebbing now.

You breathe through your mouth, not your nose. You force your lips into the mouthpiece's rim, smile with your cheeks, and buzz, like spitting out a bug. No valves, just your breath, and your breath must come from down real low.

Take the longest, lowest breath you can, the deepest one. Pull the muscles of your abdomen tight. Stand now on the wet earth beside the wet rock and face the endless, fluent river and imagine he is with you, behind you, his arms over your arms, his hands on the muscles you are tightening. Imagine he stands behind you and you blow, and a C comes out, then a B.

The letters of the alphabet of song.

Eighth note to a quarter note, and again a C. Hold the C. Just hold on, please. Just stand there, with Peggy, your heat behind her, your hands down low. Stand and do not leave her; it will be a shattering if you are not where I put you.

This, the fermata. This, the place in between.

Exhale.

Now inhale.

Now breathe.

The next sigh is—

Time running short, ahead of itself. Time running, and where is the girl, who will bring her near?

A box brings her near, the girl who is a woman now whispers, to the page. A box, and all these years.

It must be her hour approaching.

Soon the cancer will lose its battle and she will win the war. Her song playing until the needle strikes the dead wax on the run-out and time grows hitched and notched.

There's nothing —

Just those last few days in that year that was, days she wills herself to resurrect, as if this were Sunday morning. What has to happen, and what did. Why after that, and for decades afterwards, she mounted her own fierce best defense, which was forgetting. It was as if the year that was had been surgically struck from the flesh of her life. As if there isn't so much love for losing.

Holding her dark in the dark. Firming her mouth, tight. Allowing the numb dumb tick of her heart to keep tocking. The way we do, when we're surviving. The self-acting mule is a heartless machine. It goes up and down and up and down and never sees what's coming. When the bobbin grows fat, it is doffed by the doffer and tossed into a wooden cart and wheeled away and far away. You watch it trail off atop the heap of other bobbins until it's gone, unconditionally gone, except sometimes, out on the street, a dark-haired girl in a khaki-colored sweater passes, and she seems vaguely familiar. Tufts of yarn fuzz in her hair. A book in her hand, the size of her palm. A chap on her lips, because she's been practicing.

You play the bugle?

The prowl of the ambient world has trailed off toward a harbor she can't see, or a ship, big as a city. Either way, she knows what's coming.

No basketball catching a basketball rim. No gull dropping its feather from its perch on an overhead wire. No bottle of Alka-Seltzer being reunited with its lid. No new in the mew of the calico across the street, how many days have passed, where did that cat go?

If her husband is asleep down the hall, his sleep is a vast unvoiced kingdom. If he is sitting there beside her she can't hear the words he's speaking.

She would like a glass of water. Please.

She would like to sit and drink a glass of water.

She would like someone to lift the shade, for it is so dark, is night always this dark colored?

She would like someone to lift the silver brush to her head and lift the hair from her scalp that has been loosened. Or is this dreaming?

Betty—

She whispers.

Boop—

Dan?

Here comes the end, she struggles to say—

of September.

No. It *is* the end, measure its throng—two-dozen blocks long, down Broad Street. City Hall is submerged by the cavalcade of patriots. There are signs five times the height of any man. There are the high, hard flaps of flags wrestling with the breeze. There are canons on wheels, are the canons battle-ready? Soldiers with all their bayonets slashed across the shoulders of their uniforms, some of the men on crutches or touching the air for the lost half of an ear, or favoring the arm flopped in a sling. Floating biplanes. Model Ts. Brewster Town Cars. Trumbulls. The well-suited representatives of the female auxiliaries. The tall white socks, the clean white caps, the polish of the killing machines hoisted, everything is hoisted, upon the shoulders of the Navy.

Thousands of. Tens of thousands of. Two hundred thousands of. In the crush and cram—she'll read the numbers later, in the five-day-old newspaper, when everyone will blame the Fourth Liberty Loan Parade of September 28, 1918 for the things that happen next; she tries to remember what it was to be her before she knew what happened next.

The rumor is that John Philip Sousa has brought his band to play the hurrahs. The atmosphere is the Kaiser losing. The truth is the AEF has gone on the offensive in Flanders, Belgium. That the American men are regaining ground in the Fifth Battle of Ypres. That, just two days before, on September 26, the U.S. forces launched their attack on the Meuse-Argonne. The truth is that men will die in the glory of it all. That the air they will breathe will be mustard gas toxins.

Here are the widows. Here are the sisters. Here are the mothers of sacrifice. Marching. Here is the beating of drums. Here it comes, down Broad, the biggest and the best parade.

It's when the movement of the throng is whistled to a halt that the fast-talking, guilt-wielding bondsmen rush the street. They divide the Boy Scouts from the aero-floats, the war-returned from the stay-at-homes to sell their bonds. These are bucks for Uncle Sam. These are greenbacks tilled from the good and patriotic folk of the Workshop of the World. This is your civic duty. This is your pride. These are the signs that are passing:

If you can't fight your money can

Put your hand in your pocket before Germany does

Will you lend Uncle Sam Fifty Dollars?

Enlist or Invest

Go claw the fist of savings from the toe in your darned sock and give a little help to the cause. Come be pleased with what you shall receive, in exchange for your giving: a Liberty Loan button with a ribbon. Pin the button to your collar. Wear it. Proud. Be satisfied with the sacrifices you'll be making. Such a good American you are.

Peggy watches the pandemonium from the highest stone step of the Textile School at Broad and Pine. She scans the hordes for a sighting of him, though she knows he hasn't come. He is not among the injured. He has not been regained. *I don't remember worsteds.* But still she stands, his school behind her, his bugle in her hand. If she sees him she will blast a note and hold it long. *Fermata.* If she sees him, he will find her, because he will know, she remembered—didn't she?—to tell him that she'd wait for him for as long as it took, until he returned to his future.

It's Lani she sees now in the crowd. Lani with October way out before her. Lani with her Liberty Loan buttons punched straight through her collar, a placard painted bright and special for this day, with a Lani flourish:

All Hell to the Kaiser

She is beautiful, Peggy realizes, seeing her at this sudden distance. Her chin is candid. Her profile is blunt. She holds her head high on a pale, tall neck, the only stretch of slender on her body. Her dress will split with the child inside, and yet she floats, just like a bi-plane.

"Old-fashioned Influenza,"

he called it. The facts were provocative, but he ignored them. The evidence was a crescendo force: The men gone blue in Kansas. The British Grand Fleet stoppered. The Germans siphoning off a brutal June offensive when the soldiers called up to the killing fields began to drop dead, among rats, among flies before they could even so much as sling their bayonets to the frayed cloth of their shoulders. Blood in their ears, in their eyes, in their swallow. Their bodies speed-morphing into poison.

The sick people of the city of Boston. The overcome and dying in the wooden barracks and mess halls and Vaudeville theater of Camp Meade. The shadow of death at Camp Dix. The pause on the shipping of more fighters, army boys and Hello Girls too ill to board the floating cities. The six hundred men of uniform tucked into their sick beds at the Philadelphia Naval Yard, where the nurses, too, were fevering. The two sailors who died there. Then the twenty. Then—

Policeman Dead from Influenza | Epidemic in City Assuming Serious Proportions—118 New Cases in 24 Hours | Soldier Also Dies Here

the Philadelphia *Evening Bulletin* reported on page eight of September 28, including in its reporting the wise attestations of Dr. Wilmer Krusen himself, the city's public health director, the man who decided to look straight past his own worry: "If the people are careless thousands of cases may develop and the epidemic may get beyond control."

If the people are careless. Krusen said. His cautionary tale appearing in the page-eight newsprint smudge of a paper that Peggy wouldn't read for many days, and by then it was too late, for what had happened happened. *If the people are careless.* Explain, then, how it was the good doctor himself who insisted that the Liberty Loan extravaganza go on. The good doctor who refused to entertain the protestations arising from more circumspect but less powerful quarters *It's dangerous, it's deadly, stop the show.*

The show went on. Two hundred thousand Philadelphians crushing two miles of Broad Street. The spit flying above the brass bands and gold chevrons. The shoulder-to-shoulder of the industrial proud showing off their industrial wares. The juddering howitzers and the howling affirmations, the heavy-footed politicians who did not appear to be honoring the Meatless Mondays, the Wheatless Wednesdays, the god-awful rationing of sugar. Sweet-potato gingerbread for them? Peggy didn't think so. Bean loaf? Apple Brown Betty? Not a chance, Peggy had thought, always a will for the rich in their ways.

The women auxiliaries were out there marching. The trumpet players and the bassoonists. The widows and a cadre of General Pershing's wounded. The Red Cross and the doughboy knitters, the miles and miles of yarn. The tufts of loose yarn, like confetti. And the boys and the girls in their Sunday best had been squeezed to the front of the spectator lines to cheer on the Naval Yard finest, the very men who were—they did not know, they did not believe that they were dying—harboring the infection in their lungs, exhaling it out to the air, so thick, above the crowds.

Do your best, carry on, let the show go on, don't stop the show. The desideratum of the Liberty Loans, some 259 million dollars worth, and nobody need panic. Stalwart optimism is a metaphor for cheer. All hands on deck, and carry on.

It was because word of the disease had leaked by way of reporters in Madrid that the thing got its name, the Spanish flu—the journalists taking it upon themselves to send the news out over the wire. Something more deadly than the war itself was refusing to surrender, and the people—the reporters thought, though the politicians didn't—must know.

The thing had no domicile; it recognized no borders; it was belch of heat, eruptions of bloody blood and mucous. It was girlfriends and children and farmers and aristocrats, the young and healthy being the most-sought-after roost of the virus. How luscious youth was, how quick to succumb. How quickly the thing reveled in its own greed, spreading from breath to breath, from corpse to mourner. Some died within hours of the first fiery pulse. Some died moaning for their mothers.

The Spanish flu was as Spanish as the sunset was American, but that didn't matter. It was the Spanish flu now, and by the end of the weekend that had begun with the drawn-out bang of a parade, with the raining down, from some false heaven, of the thousands of Liberty Loan flyers, Philadelphia's Bureau of Vital Statistics was reporting 39 new cases of influenza. By Monday, Miss Maude Sproule, a vocalist with the Philadelphia Orchestra, was in the headlines, dead, and a quarter of the soldiers at the Frankford Arsenal had taken ill, and just one day later, October 1, "the hospitals of Philadelphia [were] crowded to the doors," according to the good doctor, Wilmer Krusen, the man who'd had a choice to make and chose the war over the people of his city.

Close the schools, the call went out by Thursday. Close the churches. Close the theaters, the dancehalls, the boxing arenas, keep the saloons in business for maybe whiskey is the antidote, maybe whiskey will become the only medicament for the hordes of dying souls.

No one was to visit the sick.

The sick, if they are dying, are best left to die alone. Their bodies already littering the streets, for the one morgue was full and the mass of coffins had been sent overseas, and the ranks of doctors and nurses were growing ever more thin; they were haggard faces on disinfected trolley cars. The police dispensaries were taking patients because the hospitals were full. The rich were turning their parlors into sanctuaries for the dying. But by Saturday some seven hundred were dead, and it was October. It is October. The baby is coming.

Lani.

Peggy wakes to the sound of her trouble. Through the open window, from within the bruise of the night it comes—Lani's voice, a low-pitched roil of bewilderment and hurt.

"No, no," she's saying. "No. Baby. Wait."

Peggy startles from the bed. Stands. Finds her feet caught in the knot of the thin white sheet that Ma, restless in the night, had kicked to the floor. Peggy will wash the dirt from this sheet weeks from now, submerging the sound of her sobs in the slapping commotion of the Triumph Rotary Washer. She will remember herself in the tangle, in the crucible of the stopped moment, the worst of it all yet to come, but not yet come. Then time springs forward and Peggy is there, at her own window, thrusting her head out over the moon-cast street and calling for her best friend: "Lani?"

"Can you?" Lani cries. "Please?"

Peggy grabs Pops's old night coat from the hook on the back of the bedroom door. She pushes her arms through the brown bells of the sleeves, ties its slim modesty around her waist, the hem of her white sleeping dress hanging lower than the coat. Her feet bare. She wakes Ma, who is asleep at last, with a quick touch on the shoulder, a kiss on the cheek. "It's time," she says. "Lani needs us."

Ma blinks in the dark. She turns to face the moon. She doesn't understand, for she's in the tail-end of a dream, but now Peggy says it again, and Ma is upright, her feet on the floor. She snaps the night lamp on. She finds her nearest tunic, her oldest skirt, her stockings, her shoes. She calls for Harry who has heard the rustling about and who stands now at the bedroom door in his work shirt and trousers, his uncombed hair tall on his head and wild. Like a black sheep, Peggy thinks. Like yarn before it's yarn. A thought she'll remember thinking years on, when her mind unreels the year she had tried so hard to forget.

"It's Lani," Ma tells Harry. "We're going to need you." Jennie gone on this night to a girlfriend's house, breaking the new rule of propriety to help the girl's dying cousin.

They chase their shadows down the stairs, through the house, down the stoop, over the dark slash of the street, to the threshold where the widow is waiting, the door behind her flung wide. "Hurry," she says. "Please." More words in a row than Peggy can remember the widow ever previously saying, and when Peggy pauses, Ma flies past her, up the stairs. "Come along now, Lani," Ma is already saying, with the calmest version of herself—words she must have heard herself at least nine times before. Ma's nine babies. Too many to keep track of. Peggy telling the story. Peg. The night that becomes dawn.

Peggy hears the slow slosh of water in a pail—the widow on the steps, now down the stub of the hallway, coming. She watches Harry take his place by Lani's pillow, his big hands forming a softer place for her head. It's as if Harry has done this very thing before—as if Harry has spent private time with Lani, cupping her head in his hands, listening to her blue-streak talk, Lani on her broad back, talking—and again Peggy pauses, wonders, watches her brother, sees how his touch calms the moaning down, the gibberish Lani was making with her tongue. "Isn't she early, though," Lani grunts out, worried, but Ma says that babies know what they want, they carry their own clock, look how eager, Lani, your baby is to meet you.

"Oh," Lani moans. "My sweet Lord Jesus." Pounding the thin mattress with her right fist, and Peggy takes that hand, that warm, warm hand, and Lani calms again, squeezes a crack out of Peggy's bones.

"That's your contractions, Lani," Ma says. "The baby coming." She adjusts the sheet over Lani's raised knees. Makes a tent of it, a private place for just Ma and the baby.

Lani rides the force of the birth, the waves. Ma stays where she is, at the bottom of the bed, no time to get to a doctor now, to a midwife or a nurse, and besides, the hospitals in the city are jammed, the beds all spoken for. This will be Ma's business now, her body thinking for her, remembering how it was, Peggy imagines, when Pops paced the parlor and Ma's ma did the birthing work—the first three babies coming too fast for any midwife to attend.

"The three of you," Pops liked to say, in telling the story, "in such eternal hurry."

"You're doing just fine, Lani," Ma says, and here comes another contraction.

"Hell to the Kaiser," Lani says, jerking forward and then flopping back, popping another bone in Peggy's hand. The heat of Lani's hand.

"Beg her pardon," the widow says. Peggy had forgotten about the widow, standing there.

"It's not a worry," Peggy says.

"It hurts, it hurts so bad," Lani says.

At the head of the bed, Harry is singing, a low, low hum, one of the dancing tunes, something silly, the best he can do to calm Lani. Every now and then he uncups one hand and touches Lani's forehead, and sends a look to Ma, standing at the foot of Lani's bed.

Ma knows. Ma understands.

"Peggy," she says. "You take a cool rag to Lani's head."

The widow goes off to fetch a rag, to cool it with clean water. "Here," she says, returning out of breath, leaving the dabbing to Peggy. The widow follows Ma's instructions. She is the help she can be, her gratitude in her obedience, her worry in the deep furrows of her brow, in the rictus of her lips.

Harry is watching the clock on the nightstand now, counting the distance between the high waves of Lani's labor, which are coming quicker and in perilous earnest. Ma has asked him to do the counting; "That'll be your best job yet, Harry," so that Peggy wonders again about Harry and Lani, and about what Ma might know and what Peggy doesn't. Peggy dabs the clean cool cloth to Lani's brow again, feels the heat of Lani's skin up through her fingers.

She catches Harry's eyes. He nods. She looks down across the tented sheet to Ma, but Ma won't catch her eye, won't give Peggy the news Peggy does not want, the unbearable, unthinkable affirmation.

The widow paces. Back and forth over the oval rug that was the fiercest shade of maroon you ever did see, Lani once said, when Peggy was sitting beside Lani on Lani's bed, reading Emerson out loud from a Little Library. Right in the square middle of Peggy's reciting Lani had said it, apropos of nothing that Peggy could imagine. "Before Pa died, the rug was maroon. And then he died and it changed hue. Overnight, Peggy. Imagine."

Now the rug is dusty rose and a geometry of the shadows that flutter according to the projections of the room's solitary lamp and Ma's moving back and forth within the light. That was the first thing Ma had done, when she'd arrived in Lani's room. Moved the night stand and then the lamp so that Ma could see the business best. Then Ma had moved the cradle with its bed of feathers against the farthest wall, near the door, so that no one in their ministrations would trip and fall, have problems of their own. An accident is the last thing a birthing baby needs. Or a birthing mother with a fever.

Ma says she can see the crowning of the baby's head. "Dark haired, she'll be," Ma says.

Lani moans. "I'm hot," she says. "Burning up." Her words sound like they come from a tongue stuck up on the roof of her mouth. Her breathing is erratic, wet. Her eyes are wild.

Ma casts a quick glance toward the head of the bed. Harry lays his hand again over Lani's forehead. Nods, but Lani can't see him. Ma asks Peggy to trade places with her now, to unclasp her hand from Lani's hand, so that Ma can lean over Lani in the short beam of light and take her own look at the heat in Lani's face. She presses her hand to Lani's forehead. The heat has a hint of the sinister.

"Would you," Ma says to the widow, taking her place at the foot of the bed. "Open the windows."

"Both of them?" the widow asks.

"Yes," Ma says. "Both."

When the widow turns to go, Ma shakes her head. Back and forth: *No.* Waiting for Lani's eyes to close before she does, a gesture meant only for her daughter and son. A sign. Harry leans back and then leans in. Peggy looks from Ma to Lani, feels the wave coming on of another contraction, Lani losing herself in the pain.

"Hell to the Kaiser. Hell to the—"

The shadows scatter toward the corners of the room, scatter back in. The rug turns another shade of rose, and Peggy can't imagine how much time has passed, how long it has been since she'd first heard Lani moaning, though when she looks up to the open windows she sees that the moon has gone and a soft light has set in. She hears a single newspaper being tossed from one stoop to the next. She hears a door open down the street and knows the door belongs to Hannah, for now she hears the sound of a stick of chalk being pressed to the street in the service of rectangle. One rectangle above another, and now the pitch of a stone to this block of South Twenty-third.

Hannah, Peg wonders now, in her remembering then. What became of Hannah?

Harry counts the time faster now, the in-between of pain. Peggy holds Lani's hand, dabs Lani's brow, but Lani's fist is releasing its fury, giving in. Peggy says, "Crack me a bone now, Lani," but Lani can't. Ma says "*Now. Now, Lani,*" and "How pretty your girl's hair will be," and "Curls, Lani. She'll have a world of them." But Lani's only half listening now, Lani is slipping into another, darker world, a hopelessness, a mourning, for Lani knows. Lani knows. She doesn't need the Finleys to tell her. She is glad the Finleys haven't.

Don't say it. Don't.

"Ma," Peggy whispers. "Lani's shaking." She is so hot. She is so cold.

"October's coming," Ma says. "October's ready," and now she asks Lani to push, and Lani doesn't. "It's your time," Ma says louder, and Lani groans. "Do this," Ma says, "for your baby."

"Please," Peggy says, the only word she has, for if she says more than that, every word will be a sobbing.

"*Now*, Lani," Ma says. "You can do it, Lani." And Harry hums a little louder, then he stops. He wipes the tears from his eyes and brings his mouth near to Lani's ear and whispers words that Peggy will never hear, but Lani does. Lani opens her eyes and braces herself and pushes with every last might she has, every bit of strength being a woman is, being a fighter like Lani. Lani is.

Here comes the baby now. Here comes the wailing of the child. Here comes the dawn, and it's the widow, crying.

The official

weekend count is 5,561 cases. Some 175,000 people in the city now are stricken. Six hundred twenty-nine have died in just the last two days. One is Peggy Finley's best friend, Lani, who changed her last name to Smith. One is Lani's baby, who lived two days long, who had been christened Harry October Smith.

October 30, 1969

This is the sigh.

This is the short sigh.

This is the long sigh.

This is the hard turbulence,

then just the sigh.

Lean into the sigh, she thinks. It's—

time.

But wait.

There is the last day to remember.

Among my—

There is the song coming back.

— souvenirs

There is the afternoon—

Beside her. The river, flowing. The end of November, and so cold. The eleventh hour of the eleventh day of the eleventh month all behind her, all black inches in the headlines that have been passed from stoop to stoop, though they're still counting the dead overseas, and the dead in her own city, and no one even knows, no one can guess, that the worst of the dying is yet ahead. She does not know, she cannot guess, that Ma and Harry will recover from the harsh wrack of the influenza but not survive the fire sixteen years hence. That Harry will fall asleep with his cigarette lit and his hand over his heart. That Ma will rush the inferno to save him. That she will not save him, or herself.

Needless to say that was a traumatic time for the whole family, her niece will write in the biography she writes that the granddaughter will read unimaginable years hence. The news in a box, carried stoop to stoop, at last.

Now, by the river, Peggy wears Lani's old sweater beneath her own emerald sweater, which makes her warm enough. Her pockets are two beds of feathers and a single pale-blue letter, the boy's last, postmarked France. She is seventeen years old, has had a birthday. She carries his bugle in one hand. It is late in the day, the dark is rumbling on, and the future is the past.

No one near, or no one near, as my grandmother, taking a long sigh now, remembers. She plants the soles of her laced-up, second-hand Hirsch-Ullman high-tops, polished just this morning with a buffing cloth, on her own flat rock. She puffs her cheeks. She lifts her hand. She presses the rim of the brass mouthpiece to her lips. A single note. A glorious fermata. The only song that's left, her final breath. And now from across the river comes the trumpet call of the silver elephant—long and rich and honorable, honor her, I wish to honor her, this story is my chance. There will not be, for me, many more chances.

She finds another long sigh of a note in her lungs. She breathes, she bugles, again. The silver elephant rises up, on his hind legs, and unfurls his trunk, and answers. River bank to river bank, bugle to trunk, a song. One note. One note. One shorter note. No note. No note at all.

And now there it is, *shhhh.* Now look at this, at all those feathers rising from her pockets, all the roving lifting from the dark curls of her hair. All the birds in all their colors in a circle now above her, *and the notes are almost articulate.* And above the birds the sky is blue, and into the blue she goes.

Blue

You traded four loosies for three sheets of paper, each one a pale shade of sky. Two boiled plum puddings for a pencil, and one Corn Willie for a pencil that worked. Lance Corporal Oswald was the last fellow's name, the one with the better stub of lead. He was a trenchmate of yours with particular affection for Crumbs, so much so that he kept Crumbs in his pocket while you wrote your letter out. Both of you standing up like most of the rest of the men, your backs pressed to the rough dirt wall, though to write the letter you had to turn and use the earth itself as backstop, you had to forget that tomorrow you'd be over the top, *Over the top, Men*, like you'd practiced.

Your boots were sunk into three inches of muck. You marched in place when you remembered how, else you'd be sucked by the muck and unable to run when the shelling came, the shrapnel.

You hadn't had a shower for weeks, except for what the rain had dumped on you. You weren't the worst thing that smelled. What smelled worse was the bloat of the sacrificed horses and men, the casual arrangement of the latrines, the decay despised by the damnable flies, the rot in the mouth of the men losing teeth. You'd lost two yourself, in particular the one in the front, so that now the space in between is a canyon. What would she say, you thought, what would she say, if she'd seen. How might you explain it to her, what a man does in war, what a man becomes?

You might say the Meuse-Argonne, but where is that to her? *Verdun.* You might say that it was you they called on to scout the corpsed craters and barbed wire of Dead Man's Hill ahead of zero hour. How they sent you out into the desolate dark and you didn't know what you were walking on and there were hardly any stars to make your map on, but you went, because when you are asked to go you go, no matter who asks you. Anyone in immediate charge is a basic rookie just like you. General Pershing calls his blustering shots from his distance, gives the orders out to the city men and farmers, the miners and the dreams of the AEF, his doughboy men with hardly any training and less ammunition and no cover from the pillboxes and gunners up high on Little Gibraltar.

No cover. No turning back. The communication trench too far distant for you to take any comfort in the hope that calls for help will be received. The supply base even further, the field hospitals, the blown-out stone houses of the early parts of the war. The roads were impassable and bloody. The trains were sliding off their loose light rails. You had what you'd come with—two hundred rounds, live bombs, emergency rations, some water that wasn't trench water, a coat for the rain, the loosies you'd traded. Now three sheets of paper. Now a pencil stub that worked.

You haven't slept since that last night in the choke of the hold of the *Leviathan*. You haven't stopped since those first nights in Brest, where your welcome party was a crowd of men in an abattoir that had been made over for the purpose.

An abattoir, somebody said. Making a joke of it.

You think Crumbs has gone deaf with all the noise of war, the vast commotion, the colossal interludes of waiting for what you can't imagine will be next. Practice your gas mask. Practice your gunning. Practice sleeping in the mud, but you don't sleep. You haven't. You walk. You keep on walking. You carry the weight of your pack through the rubble remains of French villages, between the trees hollowed and blackened by lead. You worry that your legs are so dead tired now that they won't run you fast enough when the German bullets start coming, they're coming, you won't believe when the first one nicks you on the knee just a few hours from now how many bullets there are, how they keep coming, how your knee feels no pain, your shoulder neither, now your ear, your heart, and how you won't even hear the bullets coming after that, and how glad you'll be, a joy in it, almost, that you left Crumbs back in the trench with Oswald. Crumbs, along with your letter for Peggy.

The zero hour coming. The *Over the top, Men. Over the top*. It was all just a drill at Meade. Just something to do in between dragging your cots into the air at dawn and standing your tallest five foot seven inches in salute and honoring the Star Spangled with a hum and sloshing the kit after coffee and rolls so it'd be sanitary for cucumbers and onions and lima beans, and in between that learning the handling of the gun. *Keep your rifles nice and clean, Men.* What were they even speaking of? There's not a button on any uniform in the trench that isn't caked with mud. There's not a roll of latrine paper. There's not a clean square inch on the duckboard.

Somebody says they've seen Brigadier General William J. Nicholson, leader of this 157th Infantry Brigade, holding half an apple in one hand. Somebody leans his shoulder against yours and says, apropos of—

the idea of an apple. The sudden ambrosial memory of your father's market stand, the Reading brats, the thunderous approach of the trains overhead. And now the first time you looked up and saw her, Peggy Finley, a girl seeing you beneath your cap. She wasn't a girl to flirt with. She was a girl to know. When she read out loud there was nothing in the entire Workshop of the World but the sound of the story and how close you sat to her. Her hair was thick curls. Her neck was alabaster. She was a whizzer, that Peggy Finley of the Finleys, and when you walked beside her she was taller than you, which gave you a view of the uplift of her chin, the angle it cut in your city.

No girl but her. No other hand to hold but the hand that found yours in the carved-out tunnel of the Alps at Willow Grove, which was dark except for the pretty grottoes, which was dark but for the scenery somebody had gone and painted, as if life were one amusement park.

Remember that? you write in your letter.

Remember us, you write, removing now the question mark, scrubbing it out with the stub of your pencil.

Tomorrow in the dark you will hoist your body and your rifle and your rounds over the top, and you will run toward the craters, across the buried pale gray-green uniforms of the ancient muck, across the abandoned leather of the horses, down and across the cratered shells, for it will be the zero hour, and the Germans on the hill will be ready.

Tomorrow.

But for now, with this stretch of empty left on the pale-blue page before you, you remember, and you write, another hour.

It's early November before the year that this is, and you're stoop-sitting with Peggy, outside the house on South Twenty-third. Harry's come in, and Jennie's gone out, and Ma and Pops are in the parlor, dancing, the Victrola needle ready to ride to its dead wax.

For once Lani's not talking her blue streak overhead.

For once the neighborhood kids aren't scrabbling.

It's just Peggy in her emerald sweater leaning back, catching the bit of chill sun on her chin, and it's just you, looking at Peggy, for the long-glance forever of it. It's just you now telling her a story about worsted. How, in carding the stuff, you must get the fibers nice, smooth, and straight, quoting the book you love. Nice, smooth, straight, and parallel. How, in making a sliver you're not wanting for bulk, you're wanting for a good long line, you're wanting endurance. How worsted will always be the finest in wool, and how Peggy will always be finer.

You write all this in the space that's left, remembering the wrist that wears the roving.

The promises you wished to keep.

Acknowledgments

Margaret Finley D'Imperio died on October 30, 1969, when I, her granddaughter, was nine. She was a great love of my life. She was a mystery. I was entrusted, as a teen, with her pearl necklace, and I wore it every day, until, while playing with my son at a playground by a creek, it fell away. An unbearable second losing.

Decades later, my brother arrived one Thanksgiving with a box that included a handful of long-lost pages—family genealogy, notes from my mother's cousin. The box had been left abandoned in a stranger's closet. It was discovered, brought to us. My Aunt Miriam's few spare pages suggest the contours of my grandmother's life. Her favorite song. Her employment at Fleisher's at Twenty-sixth and Reed (though not, it seems, in the year 1918). Her peach chiffon wedding dress. *Tomorrow Will Bring Sunday's News* begins with truth. It extends through fiction. For a long time, as I wrote, I thought it was a novel-in-memoir. Instead it is a Philadelphia story. A back-then story. A right-now story. A story of loss and of endurance.

In writing this book I turned to a number of sources.

My Philadelphia, textile, and Spanish flu sources included *Still Philadelphia: A Photographic History, 1890-1940* (Frederic M. Miller, Morris J. Vogel, Allen F. Davis); *Philadelphia: Portrait of an American City* (Edwin Wolf 2nd); *Forgotten Philadelphia: Lost Architecture of the Quaker City* (Thomas H. Keels); *Insight Philadelphia* (Kenneth Finkel); *The Encyclopedia of Greater Philadelphia; More Deadly Than War: The Hidden History of the Spanish Flu and the First World War* (Kenneth C. Davis); Grey Gal's History of Fleisher's Yarn Company; *Textile World Journal;* the online publications of the Smithsonian, Science Museum Group, and *Pennsylvania Heritage; Woolen and Worsted Spinning* (Forgotten Books); *The Pennsylvania Museum and School of Industry, Circular of the Philadelphia Textile School, Broad and Pine Streets; The Philadelphia Tribune, The Philadelphia Inquirer, Philadelphia Daily News,* and *Public Ledger;* The *Philly History Blog;* and "Life Was a Lark at Willow Grove Park (a 1991 documentary). My thanks to Nick Okrent, coordinator and librarian for the Humanities Collections at the University of Pennsylvania, Van Pelt-Dietrich Library Center, for picking up the phone when I called and answering my question so quickly and completely.

In addition to podcasts, films, and other sources, my understanding of World War I was advanced by *America's Great War: World War I and the American Experience* (Robert H. Zieger); *The Story of the Great War: History of the European War from Official Sources* (Francis J. Reynolds, Allen L. Churchill, Francis Trevelyan Miller); The U.S. World War One Centennial Commission; *Fort George G. Meade: The First 100 Years* (M.L. Doyle, Sherry A. Kulper, and Benjamin D. Rogers); The U.S. Army Center of Military History; Hoboken Historical Museum; *Under the Lorraine Cross* (Arthur H. Joel); and the essential Log Cabin Memorial—Veterans 314th Infantry Regiment A.E.F.

For insight into my grandmother and life on Guyer Avenue long before I was born, I turned to my beautiful and beloved Aunt Carol, one of my mother's dearest friends, who shared remembrances over lunches, who read a very early draft, and whose unqualified love has steadied me across all our decades now.

For her expertise in writerly things, I sent earlier pages of this manuscript to the fabulous, witty, and wise writer Judy Goldman, who asked questions that made this story so much better than it was. For her whisper of *keep going*, I thank the brilliant, steadfast Alyson Hagy, who is capable of reading just a handful of pages and understanding my intent, and whose own worlds of words are masterfully instructive.

To my son, Jeremy: My deepest love and admiration for the wisdom you bring to every conversation and dream. You live your life with integrity. You are forever teaching me. To my husband, Bill: Thank you for being as utterly, irreplaceably wonderful as you are, for the oil painting that graces the cover of this book (and your cover design that settles your art into place), and for standing at my side through this long journey of books and their making. It hasn't always been easy. You don't walk by or past.

Thank you, S. J. Williams, for the line-by-line grace of your intelligence, your extraordinary care, your long glance over the shoulders of these sentences. Thank you, Heide Rainey, for the design of the interior pages. And greatest thanks of all to Jessie Williams Burns, who read these pages within days of their arrival at Tursulowe Press, who sent a note of readerly generosity that buoyed and affirmed, and who invited me into her life and home—a place where I have felt blessed and welcome ever since. This book is our book (and Lupo's, too). Our friendship is forever. For every sisterly moment, for every shared sorrow, laughter, joy, and hope, for what we've made together, for the past that holds us and the present moment we are, yet, fighting for, I am and will always be beyond grateful.

Beth Kephart, a National Book Award finalist, is the author of nearly 40 books in multiple genres. She is a memoir teacher, a widely-published essayist, and a paper artist as well as a winner of a National Endowment of the Arts grant, a Leeway grant, a Pew Fellowship in the Arts grant, and numerous other awards. *Tomorrow Will Bring Sunday's News: A Philadelphia Story* is her first novel for adults. Find her words and art on her Substack, The Hush and the Howl.

www.ingramcontent.com/pod-product-compliance
Lighthing Source LLC
Chambersburg PA
CBHW032305130425
25082CB00009B/518